ONCE BENEATH
THE STARS

R. S. LENTIN

Turn the Page
PUBLISHING

Although portions of this novel are derived from real events,
each character, including those that are well-known, is fictional,
a composite drawn from several individuals and from imagination.
The events, locales, dialogue and scenes that figure in the narrative
are products of the author's imagination and are used factitiously.

Published by Turn the Page Publishing LLC
P. O. Box 3179
Upper Montclair, NJ 07043

LYRIC PERMISSIONS
INCLUDED IN APPENDIX

LIBRARY OF CONGRESS CATALOGING IN PUBLICATION DATA
Lentin, R. S.
Once Beneath the Stars / R. S. Lentin

ISBN: 0-983-21480-9
ISBN 13: 978-0-983-21480-9

Library of Congress Control Number 2011921463

PRINTED IN THE UNITED STATES OF AMERICA

Set in Garamond 3
Cover Design by Mark Delbridge, Delbridge Designs
Editors — Cari Kraft and Stacey Delbridge
Permissions by Kenneth Higney, RICH OLGA, INC.

ACKNOWLEDGEMENTS

Anything I do well, I don't do alone, even writing a book. As a Director in a law firm, I've always kept my team close at hand, valuing the contributions of each individual necessary to get the job done. For those managers who lived through the labor and birth of this book, namely, Barbara Harper, Gerry McDonnell, Ailine McLaughlin, Barbara McGee, Mary Hamm, Frank John, Relly Jacob and Lori Clar, thank you for your encouragement and support.

To Mom—Rose Stella, Aunt Sis—Antoinette Max, sister—Denise Moffa, and longtime friend—Linda Macht, the first readers of the manuscript, your surprise, questions and interest in continuing to turn the pages, gave me the heart to move forward. I won't forget Mom looking up from her reading and asking, "How did you learn to write like this?"

To my informal team of contributors, Penny Mitchell, Sue DiCesare, Sine Bachkocning, Silvana Cosentini, Jeff Bruce, Vicki Rimasse, Tracy Greenlee, and Linda Weisberg—you made this venture fun. To Stacey and Mark Delbridge, editor and artist respectively, your talents are evident on the pages and on the cover of this book. Kenneth Higney is "The Man" who secured the permissions for the lyrics in the book, with special thanks to Troy Schreck of Alfred Publishing. The poetic work of the musical artists contained herein add a richness to the story and I thank the artists and publishers for sharing their work. To Cari Kraft, your time, attention, interest, and creativity, made this a better book.

My daughters, Laura Lentin and Alaina Lentin, were the first to encourage me when the New York City Chapter of the Association of Legal Administrators (ALA) asked me to be Editor of the *New York New York* newsletter, launching me on this roller coaster ride of writing, editing and publishing.

A few special people from the ALA influenced my growth as a writer—Jackie Todd, Lynne Rosenthal, Nadia Wagner, Marion Grobe, the late Martha Llano, Barry Jackson, Kim Swetland, Marjorie Stein, Rita Thompson, Ken Knott and Phil Carvahlo.

There's one person not named who is the real inspiration of the book. His memory and the memory of his life, his hope, and his love, are brought to you on these pages. I like to think that what is written here is a message from his heart to yours.

Hillary said it best, "It takes a village." Thank you.

Roseann Lentin

DEDICATION

To the man who inspired the story, and who showed us how to live within the confines of our skin. Listening to you, I heard the music. Thank you.

Love,
Ro

CHAPTER 1

1993

To sleep ... perchance to dream.

Hamlet

"You're the man," Mike says, looking up from a hotel room bed, his usually resonant voice stretched thin like a high wire straining between mountains.

His brother, Tommy, red faced, swollen, holding grief in check, points his finger, tears brimming, Mike expecting the usual, "No, you're the man," the volley they threw ever since Tommy was 12 and Mike 18, coming home in a wheelchair. When Tommy became the man helping his mom and sisters with all kinds of physical tasks a kid brother shouldn't have to do with Joe away at college and Dad in the den watching TV.

Today, at 31, Tommy's face cracks and tears roll as he wags his finger, the only answer, no words, his mouth tied in a woeful smile. After traveling all day from Philly to Detroit, after arriving at the Quality Inn and checking in under fake names, after lifting Mike and tucking him in for the last leg of the mother of one way trips, all is said that has to be said. Tommy takes Mike's words and rolls them into his fist, leans over, grasps Mike's hair, and kisses his cheek smearing tears.

"Thanks, man," Mike whispers, and Tommy tightens his hold. Mike's throat is crowded with tears, his arms immobile under the sheet, but his heart reaches out to hug back.

Standing, Tommy pulls a tissue from a box on the nightstand, wipes under Mike's glasses and straightens them, leaving his own face wet. Smoothing Mike's hair like a parent, Tommy's tight smile relaxes and his eyes are satisfied. Mike thinks of all the times Tommy fixed his hair, without thinking, as if it was his own.

The familiar scent of Tommy's hands fills his nose. A working smell from a man who toils; not an earthy smell, rather a shade of sweat mixed with metal. Closing his eyes, he wants to hold it inside, bring it with him wherever he's going. The smell of kindness, selflessness, from hands Tommy lent him all these years.

"I'm goin' now," Tommy says, his nose reddening.

Mike nods and looks away, wanting Tommy to know he can leave, which he does, fast, turning and wiping his face backhand and latching the door softly behind him. The small sound echoes loudly in Mike's mind— the sound of his family finally set free from the burden of his chair, for as surely as he was wedded to it, so were they.

Tears sting but Mike blinks them back and focuses on the blank space of the ceiling—the last of hundreds of ceilings a man grounded by skin and bone sees while looking into the day and night of things. Breathing easier, he takes in the quiet room, its anonymity soothing. No emotional promise in any of the furnishings. Nothing here to latch on to, hold him on earth.

He's alone. In the dimming light, the cold Michigan air seeps through thin curtains. Talking done, praying done, Mike focuses on release from his body, dependency, and from the worry and debate about choosing death, real death, over a living death.

Pushing back in the pillow, the cold penetrates the light blanket over his jeans and long sleeved t-shirt. Mike wishes he'd asked Tommy to pull the spread up. He's glad the light is on, but his heart speeds up thinking the doctor won't show. What if he doesn't and something happens to Tommy? No one knows he's here. "Calm down, man," he says to tinny air. He glances at the door then stares through it, knowing when it opens he'll be released—finally, forever—from the bondage of his soul.

⌘ ⌘ ⌘

Everything's quiet. Hears only his breathing. Eyes rest on the hotel room's ceiling—old, two by two's. Mike knows ceilings. Most are sheet rock like the one at home, blank, unreachable, but the corky one above him now holds secrets. Mike thinks the secret about to unfold is much too grand for this non-descript room, with its desk, chairs and lamps that could be anywhere in the world.

Waiting for the doctor, he contemplates what will happen after. Wonders if he'll pass through the ceiling and drift up to the darkening sky into a sea of stars. Tries to imagine the magic of it, but he's scared thinking of hurling through space next to balls of fire. Instead, he pictures himself looking down from above watching the Doc unhook the machine, fold the wires and pack them neatly in a suitcase. He sees his body in bed, eyes closed, glasses still on. Will I regret doing this thinking I could've held on longer? Waited for a cure? Or will I feel blood again in my arms and legs no longer captive in the shell? Guess I'll find out soon, he thinks.

Gauging the distance from floor to ceiling, he estimates about eight feet. At 6'3" he could probably reach it standing on tip toe. With his height just dead weight, it's eight feet and forever to get there.

Turning to the window, the sun's rays slant long—the beginning of the end of a day that began in dark and would end in dark. He wonders what mom is doing right now. Probably cleaning up dinner, if they even ate.

Swallowing tears, he recalls this morning, when a knife sliced through his middle when his mom and sisters, Judy and Rita, hugged him for the last time. Mom's Jean Naté had filled his nose, her bathrobe soft on his cheek. After a night of torment, he wanted to sink into the robe's shoulder and hide from the day ahead, his last day, like a kid burying his face under a pillow to escape a monster.

Neither he nor mom slept last night. He'd heard the clink of silverware deep in the night, the teapot's low whistle. The small noises echoed in the slumbering house, where sounds grew brighter when lights dimmed. When he'd heard her soft knock on his door, he didn't answer and closed his eyes.

When the knob turned and the door opened, a hush of air entered like the break in a vacuum, a soft note, hanging, expectant. Pretending to sleep, he'd heard the teacup rattle when the door closed, the vacuum sealed once more. Just wanted to spare her more misery.

They had given him a sleeping pill. It didn't work. Wound like a top, he had stared at the ceiling, moonlight gray, saying goodbye to the wavy shadows etched in his mind from sleepless nights spent waiting—for morning, for relief from an itch, a cramp, or for someone to brush away a spider spinning a web between the spokes of the headboard. His last night lying in cement. In a way, he had wanted to rejoice.

But this morning at the door, with mom's arm around him, the knife severed his last vestige of resolve by cutting the seal on a cauldron, releasing flames that seared his throat. Knowing he'd never see her again, hot tears burned his cheeks when she whimpered in his ear.

Glasses askew from her arm 'round his neck in a stranglehold, their tears formed a moist seal, weaker than the one he broke through bursting into life—that time with her help to unleash him. This time her thin arm was a lifeline. The only one that could stop him. This woman who nursed him at both ends of his life, and with her age and all the work and sorrow, still unwilling to release him to death.

He had called on the athlete still living inside him, honed for action, and trained for the past 20 years to persist. He'd focused and used his mind, his only tool to cut the cord, his voice sharp and sure. "Let's go, Tommy," he had said, cutting through her arm, the command in his voice shutting out her crying, his eyes focused only on the end zone, the final hurrah.

As he had called his last play on the field so long ago in a clipped, pointed tone, so he now called this play, with Tommy his lone teammate, his center, who instead of handing him the ball, gently pulled mom's arm away, and instead of pushing through the defense, came behind him, and pushed the wheelchair through the line.

Rolling one last time from his room off the den of his parents' house, a room Dad had built but never entered, Mike thought of his friends who had gathered there to watch TV or listen to music, or the reporters who used to visit to quote him in their articles, laughing and talking about news or sports, and he wished he could've said goodbye. But he couldn't, and his insides were stale when he rolled into the van. It was all so medieval—him slinking off to die. He had wanted a party—some fanfare for his life, reputation. Instead, they'd left before dawn, in the dark, before the promise of sunrise.

As dust particles now danced in the waning rays of his last sunset, he thought about Joe, who would know by now. Tears burned imagining Joe's face when he saw the empty bed and realized the van was gone. He could see mom telling him, and Joe crumpling in her arms or raging around the house at nobody, everybody, his anger meant for Mike. For not saying goodbye.

As close as brothers could be, Mike and Joe were closer. Sometimes Mike felt he had jumped into Joe's skin and moved around in there and that's what kept him alive all these years. Every day at five, Joe would burst through the door. "Hey kid," he'd say smiling—even at 37 he still called him kid. He always brought something too, a magazine, an article to discuss, Entenmann's coffee cake or soft pretzels smothered in yellow mustard. And music—albums, back in the day. They'd listen for hours while Joe exercised Mike's scrawny arms and legs, Mike wondering how he could do it. He never asked, afraid to lodge a kernel of disgust in Joe's mind. When the covers were off his legs, he'd avert his eyes, afraid to see them so thin and gross reflected in Joe's eyes.

Tonight, glancing at the phone resting idly on the nightstand, he wanted to call, hear mom's voice, talk to Joe, set things straight. But he could only reach the phone with his eyes and his heart.

Doesn't matter anymore, Mike thinks. Joe knows how it is. They'd talked long and hard about death, Mike asking early on for help to end the pain. Pain that used to spike like fire was now beaten down to an even tone that reverberated deep, like a rumbling truck in the distance. He remembered the doctors' faces right after the accident when they'd told him some nerves were still alive—faces twisted with bad news and good—good because there was life in the nerves, bad because these particular nerves signaled pain. And those signals ran strong and true like a freight train throwing sparks on a hard turn. Pills and exercise eventually managed the pain to a slow burn, a simmering he had learned to live with. Sometimes cramps pushed and pulled at the same time. Cramps he had to outlast. And outlast them he did, many times, through sweat and music, his brother Joe talking him through.

They talked about everything, him and Joe. Tommy too, when he was older. Asked them both many times if they could help him end the pain. Thing was, talking with Joe kept the pain at bay, kept him hopeful for a cure—that he would walk again. And Tommy, well, he would listen but just shake his head and say he couldn't give him the pills.

Death became a regular topic after Jenna left a few years ago, when company dwindled 'cause he was surly, reclusive. Joe talked him through that as well. But thoughts of ending it escalated and Mike wasn't sure if he brought it up to get a reaction, to see whether they were tired of taking care of him, or whether he meant it. Then he saw the documentary on Dr. Kevorkian, and today would finally meet him.

CHAPTER 2

The blanket's not pulled tight. He's cold. Unable to shiver, he turns to the window to catch the last light of day, to imagine its warmth. His last sunset blocked by curtains.

Maybe I'll call Tommy. Looking at the door, he wonders if he's outside the room. Thirsty. Doesn't matter. Cold. Doesn't matter. I'm already dead. Been dead. And he wondered if anything he did these past twenty some years mattered.

Joe said it did. Joe said life itself is what matters—that everything has a purpose. When he said things like this, Mike would raise his arms, straight out in the one and only gesture in his bag of tricks and look at them like a question, like what the hell is the purpose of this? Joe would point out all the good Mike did with his fundraisers and how he'd helped disabled kids, how he was a role model and still an athlete 'cause only an athlete could endure like he did. But when Joe left to go home to his wife and kids, Mike would turn back to the ceiling and wait another 22 hours till Joe was back with his musings.

Last night, Mike had been restless during Joe's visit. He never lied to him before, but this wasn't really a lie. He just didn't say he was going to Michigan. Afraid Joe might stop him.

But Joe knew something was up. When he'd said goodnight, he looked Mike in the eye a little deeper, rested his hand a little longer on Mike's arm. At the door, he turned and looked back as if to ask a question, but instead opened the door and disappeared in the night. When Tommy came in later to get Mike ready for dinner, he'd needed four tissues to clean him up.

Like when Jenna left. Tommy cleaned him up after that too. Jenna's face flashes in his mind, her blond hair, long when he first saw her—a cheerleader at Bishop Tremont—short and wavy 15 years later. If he had his hands, he could have held her—close—could have run his fingers through her hair, could have held her from a marriage to a selfish man. He glances at the phone again. Guess she'll read it in the papers, he thinks.

Gray shadows fall across the room swallowing up daylight. The glare of the bedside lamp throws stark rays in a circle, blue and cold. The Doc told him he'd come after nightfall. Kind of ghoulish, but Mike understands. They can't flaunt what they're doing. After all, it'll be Mike pulling the string to release the valve. And the whole thing will be taped. Mike pictured the doc giving the tape to his lawyer, the man who helped Tommy make the arrangements. Is Tommy still here? Maybe he's talking to the doc right now, in the lobby. No, they couldn't be seen together. He's probably waiting in the rental car to make sure the doctor comes. I should have called Jenna, let her know. Does Joe know? What time is it? Where's Tommy?

A knock, soft and gentle, wavers through the slate air. The door opens breaking the vacuum, clearing Mike's mind from downward spirals. A gray haired man in a rumpled jacket stands on the threshold. He holds a leather bag—square, sturdy. Big glasses magnify the eyes Mike locks on—compassionate, sharp. The man who will bring relief ... The Man, Mike thinks.

"Hi, Doc," he says, his breath escaping in a wintry puff. "Hurry, before I change my mind."

CHAPTER 3

1973

Don't you know that you are a shooting star.

Bad Company

He's pumped. In the locker room with new teammates dressed in Wildcat red and white instead of the Knight's black and gold, the colors irked but energized him 'cause this is big news, him changing schools. First game of the season, there'll be cameras, scouts. Tying laces, a slight quiver shoots through Mike's gut. Wonder if the guys mind I'm getting all the attention after only one summer of practice with this team. Looking up at numbered jerseys on the backs of his offensive line he thinks, I don't really know these guys.

Playing for Bishop Tremont through junior year and transferring to Washington High School in June, he didn't have time to lock in loyalty like he did at Tremont, where he'd still be if the football coach didn't listen to nonsense from the doctors about a hit he took not healing. Hell, Tremont's baseball coach didn't mind when he pitched a winning season last spring.

Mike's jaw had dropped when the football coach called him in and told him in "no uncertain terms," those were the words he used, "In no uncertain terms will you play on my team against doctor's orders." The coach's finger tapped the desk in time to his words.

Mike couldn't speak, could only see Notre Dame looming large in his future. Baseball could get him there, but quarterbacking's his ticket.

"I have to play, Coach!" Mike had leaned forward in the chair.

Pursing lips the coach leaned back, "Not until the doctors say so."

Every hair stood at attention on top of Coach's military crew cut, the style he demanded of his players. Mike's eyes fixed on the hairline aware of his own hair touching his collar. Standing, Mike's chair scraped the floor. Towering over the desk, his mind worked a thousand angles but the coach's eyes stood firm so Mike turned and left the office without a word.

"Hey Murphy! You goin' soft on us?" Mike looks up at the left tackle, Gene, whose straight chin matches the line of his shoulders that are as wide as the aisle. Looks like a Knuckles or Ant'ny, not Gene.

"I'm ready." He stands straightening the waist of his uniform then reaches into the locker for his helmet. Black with a red paw print. He stares at it.

"Let's go guys!" the offensive coach yells from the doorway and the team springs into action, their spikes clicking like cattle on a dance floor.

Running from the tunnel into the bright day, Mike hears the roar of the crowd. A home game. He's played here before, but only on Sundays, when Catholic schools played, after Church and lunch. Now he's a "public" playing the game he loves on Saturday.

Driving over, his brother, Joe, who is somewhere in the stands, had turned up the radio, looked over at Mike and sung along with Chicago's *Saturday in the Park*, singing the word "Saturday" very loud. Mike knew what he meant.

The switch to Washington caused all kinds of controversy in the papers. Rival schools, Tremont and Washington were both located in Somers, PA, a quiet suburb of Philadelphia, where Mike's family, the Murphy's, lived.

The schools competed in everything—sports, band, cheerleading, and in general on neighborhood streets, where some kids go to public school and some go to Catholic. Most in Mike's neighborhood were Catholic.

For his family, the transfer had a religious impact. His Irish Catholic parents didn't like it—well Dad didn't want him playing football at all no matter where, and mom didn't like that he'd be against the Catholic school. Said he still had to go to Church.

Mike stood tall against the outrage, knowing he's doing what's best for him, not everybody else. Besides, now he's in class with girls, not holed up all day in Tremont's boys' division looking across the campus to the girls' school.

In the couple of weeks here at Washington, he's already made his place—in the hallways, cafeteria, where he's happy to see girls in jeans—not plaid uniforms with flat, nun shoes. He smiles and charms and enjoys the attention his good looks bring. Kids at Washington like that he's here— kind of like they won over Tremont.

"All right guys, huddle up." His new coach, thick gray hair combed to the side, walks into the middle of the jostling pot of boiling testosterone, the guys anxious to get on the field and show their stuff.

"You know what to do ... what we practiced," he circles hitting each one in the eye with his words. "We want the championship this year." He glances at Mike. "Let's go out there ... and get it!"

The team erupts in a crash of fists and muscles. Mike's somewhat disoriented without the mumbled prayer, all hands to the middle then breaking and running. He lags behind, adjusting his helmet, dark hair hanging below it. Three cameramen are setting up on the sidelines, one he recognizes from the *Somers Courier Times*. Two older guys wearing baseball caps and holding clipboards stand watching. Squinting, Mike tries to see insignia's but can't. He wears shaded aviators off the field to drive and stuff, but he doesn't need his glasses when he plays.

On the track in front of the bleachers, the cheerleaders swing back and forth in unison shaking pompoms—one red, one white—and kicking bare legs. Swaying black and gold skirts flash in Mike's mind. He misses the sound of Tremont's marching band, their fight song, "Go, go, go, Knights go," and the drumbeat, low and deep, when they march around the field before a game, the cheerleaders in back, moving their arms in a timed circle. One of the cheerleaders, Jenna, always caught his eye, sometimes on the field, sometimes at practice. Great legs. Wants to ask her out. Maybe I will, he thinks.

Arms pumping, Mike jogs past the goal posts where the opposing team, Upper Rockville, prances onto the field. Their blue jerseys match the sky. Mike's tall, lean frame, more suited to the mound, stands out and a few opposing teammates look over. They know who he is. Smirking, Mike faces one of the guys, number 31, a big guy with a bulldog face, and motions a couple of punches.

"Asshole," the guy shouts.

"Murphy!" Washington's assistant coach yells.

Mike smiles, running backwards with arms in an 'I surrender' gesture. On the sidelines, he loosens up, stealing glances at the stands looking for signs of black and gold. Have to be some kids from Tremont here. But faces aren't discernable in the moving sea of strangers waving red banners and cheering. Teammates offer a wide berth as he prepares, but up close their sidelong glances bring a jolt in his gut, knowing they're depending on him for the season. Nerves, man, calm down, he says to himself, shaking his arms. I got this.

Cymbals from the marching band ring out and everyone stands for the national anthem. The flag whips proudly from the middle of the field, like a soldier saluting the homeland. Helmet under his arm, hair blowing on his neck, Mike's stomach is in a knot.

Winning the toss, Washington's special team returns the kick to the 23 yard line. He's up. Running on the field, his anxiety falls away with each step of his cleats dug in the earth. He's centered, focused, as if the little holes in the ground plant him exactly where he's supposed to be. Red and white or black and gold, he's in his element. Sounds of the crowd fade as concentration adds to his composure. Focusing only on the goal line, his body takes over, every muscle honed, each practiced movement precise and clear in his mind.

Crouching in the huddle, he hears only his breathing while his heart beats steadily in his chest. Looking up to expectant faces, his deep voice is confident, sure. "Eight thirty eight, right." Clapping in unison the huddle breaks and they line up.

An easy running play, they gain two yards and break the ice of nerves. On second down, they run for another five. In the huddle, Mike feels the team's chemistry pulling together, the sidelines far away, the team in synch. He calls for a pass on third and three, and looks the receiver straight in the eye like saying, "I'll do my part, you do yours."

Bent over the center he yells to his left, "Four forty four," to his right, "Four forty four, hut, hut." And the ball is his. The leather that will bring him fame and glory. It fills his hands and he squeezes it, dropping back. The play executes perfectly, the line holding the defense giving Mike his pocket.

Finding his man, he throws to his right, a tough pass but the ball sails in a confident arch. Coming at him is 31, his blue jersey filling the sky. Mike's eyes flash to Gene off to his left. Before 31 gets to him, he's hit from behind. His neck whips back. Hears a crack. Scaring pain shoots down his back. Like a ragdoll he falls facedown, bouncing on the grass.

Electricity burns a path to his toes. A sound like air popping— pfffffffffffffffft—comes from the base of his neck and the pain disappears. Eyes closed, balloons fill his head. He's letting go, rising up, his body light and floating through the blue sky into the black.

Sunk deep, he hears his name, over and over. Someone is calling but the cushiony black is warm, enveloping him. "Mike!" Joe's voice cuts through jarring him. He crashes to earth, the smell of grass, voices, commotion. Blinking, he sees cleats everywhere.

Drifting again, closing his eyes, Joe calls him back, "Mike, Mike!" Joe's sneakers, then his knee, then his face all the way down, almost on the grass. "Mike!"

And seeing Joe makes him want to stand. To get both their faces off the ground. But his head is heavy, leaden, and there's an emptiness below his neck, as if his body still floated in the sky. And the weight of his head and the lightness of his body make him think a dark question. A question he's not ready to ask.

"I'm thirsty," Mike says.

"Ok, ok, going to be ok," Joe's strong voice belies the look in his eyes. "Hey, I need some water over here!" Joe yells behind him.

"Don't move him! Don't move him!" a man's voice yells coming closer.

"Get my helmet off ... I can't ... I can't ..." he struggles to lift his cheek from pressing into the helmet but there's no way to do it. He tries to find his arms to push up and stand but all he can do is blink.

"He needs a drink," Joe looks up. Mike sees gray slacks and sneakers next to Joe.

"The ambulance is coming. Can you hang on, son?" A man leans down. He's wearing a yellow jacket—a coach but his hair's long and Mike can't place him.

"I'm just thirsty," he says feeling a hole in his middle.

Joe runs off. Licking parched lips, Mike closes his eyes wanting to fade inside his helmet to hear only breathing like in the huddle, so he can think, call the next play.

"Here, Mike." Joe has a paper cup in his hand. He presses it so a spout aims at Mike's mouth. "Open up."

Mike catches the water in his mouth, solid gulps clinging to life, swallowing the care and concern in Joe's eyes.

"Thanks, man," Mike says when the cup is empty, the small amount of water helping but not satisfying the river he wants to swallow to fill himself up. Joe wipes Mike's mouth with his thumb, eyes tearing behind glasses.

The dark question looms large in Mike's head, like a billboard flashing. It takes up so much space he can barely see it the lights are so bright.

Mike slants his eyes up to Joe, "Am I paralyzed?" he asks, his voice tentative, testing the words on his tongue.

Joe's face answers, but words of comfort and encouragement come out of his mouth. All Mike can hear is his face.

Again and again he asks and keeps asking, as they brace his neck, lift him on a gurney, and wheel him over bumpy grass to the ambulance. No one answers, all eyes and hands focused on getting him to the hospital.

When the car speeds away, its siren blaring, Mike sees the red lights reflected in the window as the red and white stadium fades in the distance.

Two men dressed in white work to hook up an IV, the man closest to him has blue eyes like the jerseys, the sky. Head immobilized, chin strapped tight, Mike manages only a few words.

"Where's my brother?"

"He's following us to the hospital," the man answers, turning toward him with a needle the size of Wisconsin.

"What's that?"

"Just a sedative to relax you,"

"I'm ok." Mike's eyes try to stop him but the needle strikes and, not feeling it, he looks at the roof.

An ocean inside his head drowns out the siren. He asks once again, "Am I paralyzed?" his voice a monotone, not really a question, not expecting an answer. Hoping he's playing a part, like he practiced many times in his bedroom, the mirror reflecting expressions of pain, anger, delight, depending on the story. Sometimes Joe busted in finding him there with outstretched arms, deep voice exclaiming his love or reciting Shakespeare's lines from Hamlet or Macbeth, his two favorite plays. Always wanted to be on stage.

Eyes closing, he's back in the huddle—only the sound of breathing, his heartbeat. And then the ball's in his hands. He drops back, throws, then tries to dodge when the blue comes toward him. But it's too big. It fills his head wide as the sky, like a blanket coming down softly, covering him, and blocking out the light.

CHAPTER 4

A vise squeezes his head, face stuffed in a hole looking down to a beige floor. Dull pain cinches the base of his neck. Below him, a mirror reflects the ceiling; a silver pole on wheels is next to it. Thin white tubes drape down pulsing liquid. Steady beeping comes from somewhere overhead. The smell is antiseptic.

Lips dry, he pulls them apart. His forehead thuds into the cushion. Moaning, his throat burns raw. Wanting to call out, he can't. He struggles weakly trying to move his head. It's locked in.

"Mike?" A woman's face appears in the mirror, red hair under a nurse's cap. He sees her face and her shoes at the same time—white shoes, the quiet kind. "I'm Gloria, your day nurse. We're happy to see you," she says speaking in plural nurse talk.

"Where ..." the breath to form words doesn't come easy.

"You're in Morris Hospital. You've been here for two days now," she says in a chipper voice behind a tense smile.

Falling back in his mind, thoughts begin to form, memories ... the throw, the hit, pffffffft, Joe's face leaning down, sirens, the needle. The rhythmic beeps speed up.

"Calm down, Mike, I'll get your mother."

Eyes like frightened birds, he searches for arms, hands, to turn over, get his face out of this hole. Like on the field, he can't move. Pushing his chin into the cushion, he opens his mouth to take deep breaths. The beeping increases.

"Mike!" the click of small heels and heavier footfalls. "Hey, kid." Mom and Joe. Tears prick but his throat is dry. Mom's face in the mirror shows red rimmed eyes. Joe crowds next to her with a tight smile. Their shoes are underneath him—flats and sneakers. Grass stains on the sneakers. He can't see their bodies.

"Mom ..." his voice a scratch.

"Everything's all right," Joe says, his face in a knot.

Mike looks from one to the other. His eyes harden. "Don't ... bullshit ... me."

Mom's shoes click away, quiet sobs. Joe's hand touches the back of Mike's head, a small relief he can feel it.

"My throat ... turn me over, man."

Joe looks back at the door. "Have to get the doctor," he mumbles.

"Get 'em ... I'm awake ... turn me over ... get me out ...." Panic strikes realizing he's trapped. Unable to move, a thunder rolls through him, a billowing cloud gone wild, constricting his throat, choking. Beeping goes haywire. "Aaaaaaaaaaaaah!" he wails, the only release valve, his mind no longer the boss. A doctor ... needs a doctor to turn over.

"Mike!" Mom and the nurse come running.

"Steady, steady," Joe pets his head then grabs his hair. Mike hears him crying. Hears mom crying somewhere near the bed.

Face in a grimace, Mike's throat fills up and tears drip straight down, splashing briefly then puddling on the floor. His crying only comes from his head, without shaking shoulders or chest heaves. Like an open spout, it pours.

"Excuse me," the nurse who had been fumbling with the machines pushes Joe aside. She squats. Her face in front of him is round, take charge. She has tissues in her hand and wipes him up. Blows his nose. Stays with him till the beeping is even and the only other sound is mom sobbing some-where in the background.

The dark question he asked on the field is answered by the competent look in Gloria's eyes. A neutral look when she blows his nose, like it's her job, nothing more. Like she and others like her will be there for him with their tissues and consolation in the times to come. She leaves to get the doctor.

Helpless, hanging upside down, Mike sees the tips of Joe's shoes under the bed and gauges the distance. From here to the sneakers is light years, Mike thinks.

Understanding what's gone down, he assumes his role, what he needs to do to get himself and others through. He needs to be the athlete, the popular guy with a blip on his radar. Just a blip.

"Hey Joe," he calls.

Joe blows his nose and leans in the mirror. "Yea?" His voice holds tears. Black glasses frame his eyes making him look drawn, pale. He disappears from the mirror and comes down and sits cross legged on the floor.

Mike looks him hard in the face. "You look like shit," Mike says breaking the tension, his voice stronger.

Joe chuckles deep in his throat. Cracking a smile, he shakes his head and says, "It ain't been good."

"I need water," Mike says feeling like he did on the field, like he could drink for miles. That he'd suck it down and it would never fill the void. His lips are cracked, dead like, unattended.

"Hey mom ... mom, can you get the nurse? Mike wants a drink." Joe talks in soft tones like in church.

"Yes," mom sniffles, leaves the room. The beeping is still even.

"Did I make the pass?" Mike asks and they both laugh. Another small relief ... that he can laugh.

Joe leans forward. "I'll help you," he says, with a look Mike can't decipher, a mixture of telling and not telling. "We'll get you turned over. It's a whole production!" He makes a face with his eyes.

"A production, huh," Mike says.

"You're in traction," Joe reaches and touches the back of his own neck. "There's wires and stuff holding you straight."

Mike's eyes linger on Joe's, his vision clearer, sharper, like an animal trying to find a way out of a trap.

"What's the doctor say?" Mike asks, not changing his gaze.

"They don't know yet, Mike. Now that you're awake, it'll be easier for them to examine you, ask questions."

A cup is handed to Joe. Mike sees but still can't hear Gloria's shoes. "Don't drink too fast," she says, walking away.

Joe lifts the straw to Mike's lips. He drinks, long pulls on cool water soothing his throat, moistening his lips, bringing life inside. Remembering Joe giving him a drink on the field, he wonders if this is how it'd be for a while. Choking, water spills on the floor.

"Drank too fast," Joe gets up, grabs some tissues.

"Sorry," Mike says.

Joe wipes Mike's mouth and then the tiles, using a circular motion, as if cleaning the floor is the most important thing he can do, rubbing till the tissue's in pieces.

"Dad been here?" Mike asks, his mind reeling backwards to the times he'd come in from a pick-up football game, all dirty and victorious. Dad would look through lowered lids as Mike ran down the plays, Dad's eyes smoldering, as if he knew that every completed pass brought Mike closer to this goal.

"Not yet," Joe answers, the tissues rubbed to a pulp.

CHAPTER 5

Two weeks of torture. Flipped like a pancake from front to back, the bed turns over in concert with the metal and ropes holding him in place. Stretched taut, days and nights blend in the glare of fluorescent lights—12 hours facing them, 12 hours, the floor. They doped him up plenty.

Increasing the gap between "cocktails," the grip on his neck is enough to snap him into the universe and explode him into a thousand hot stars. Grinding, relentless pain rolls down from his neck into a tangle of flaming tendrils lashing left and right from the spine, enticing him to relinquish his soul to the burning and allow it to simmer in the ash.

From somewhere in hell, Mike hears screaming, a man screaming for help. Then, a soothing voice makes him open his eyes and the screaming inside his head becomes his own voice in his ears. He looks out from his pleading, hoping to see mom's face rumpled from sleep, in her nightgown, smoothing the covers and telling him to roll over, go back to sleep.

Sometimes Joe is there saying, "It's all right, it's all right" and Mike knows it isn't right, otherwise mom would be saying, "Rest now, it's only a dream."

When he's sure to die, relief comes through a needle. Then the dusk behind his eyes blocks out the fluorescents. Floating, he's released from pressure, free of the flames that lick at his limbs and fingers, as if to remind him they're there. But reminders aren't enough. He'd wake again still chained to the bed.

Skin tingles—which the doctors say is good—but it turns to gnawing. Gritting teeth, he practices endurance until he can't take it and screams for the meds. The nurses say, "Hold on, Mike. Open your eyes. Can you look at me?" Sweat pours from his forehead trying to find the athlete to push through the pain like he did to make another good throw with a spent arm.

"Please," he cries, breathless. Sometimes the doctor appears, places a stethoscope on his neck. He wants to yell, "I can feel it!" 'cause they're always asking, but he's lost in the desert and he's hot then cold and the shaking takes over. Finally the needle comes and the grip loosens and he's back in the night.

Tests of endurance become more frequent. Soon, he's able to stay awake, talk for a while till the pain comes back at him from a hundred yards, like a steam roller ready to mow him down. Trying to run, the blue jerseys again fill the sky and the roller hits him, opening a small crack in his spine separating head from toes. A hairline fissure that's as wide as a canyon.

As the weeks pass, he stays topside longer, endures quietly. But the pain can't help but creep on his face. He sees it reflected in the eyes of the nurses when they come in to check. Shortly after, relief is added to his IV and a soft darkness envelopes him, bringing him to where dreams are real, like he's walking and moving as usual. Most of the dreams are in slow motion, limbs moving fluidly, perfectly. Practicing for when he'd walk again.

Someone from the family, his mom or one of his sisters, is usually here when he wakes up, giving him water, smiling, speaking in positive verbs. Tommy comes after school and wants to help, but it's hard for him to reach over the metal bed guards that nurses say are "required." As if I can fall out, Mike thinks. He takes it as a sign of hope.

Days and nights, dreaming, waking, Mike commands his body to move. With jaw set and forehead sweating, he presses down in his mind, willing the bones to knit back together. Willing whatever had snapped inside to mend, to set the line straight from his head to his toes. "Like two bars of soap trying to stick together," the doctor had said, the bones needed magic, a magic that wouldn't come.

CHAPTER 6

The doctor stands in between the beds, his back to Mike as he fumbles in his bag while his assistant, Bill, hooks up the video camera. Both bedspreads are covering Mike, but the cold seeps through him as if he's already dead. The doctor murmurs a steady stream of information punctuated by a wide-eyed look through his big glasses. All the talk keeps Mike focused on what the doc is saying rather than what he's doing.

"Now, I have to ask a few questions before I get everything ready ...," the doc's face is buried in the bag and Mike can barely hear him. "But let's wait for Bill here to get the camera on ...." More shuffling, tubes and silver casings pulled from the suitcase, the casings clanging their death toll when they roll into each other on the bed. He places what looks like a rubber heating pad, the kind you fill with water, and some other things on the bottom of Mike's bed.

Twisting the camera onto a tripod, Bill says, "Almost ready, Doc." Bill's a big guy who keeps himself apart in a respectful way. Stays busy and lets Doc do the talking.

"Ok, ok, no hurry," Doc says as he assembles the metal into a pole that stands about five feet high next to the bed.

Mike's watching as if from afar, not feeling impatient, not feeling scared, not feeling anything really. A sense of comedy, unreality, plays in his mind. Maybe that's what the doctor intends. Mike feels at ease, like waiting for a haircut. With the doc and Bill here, the room's not as cold. Has a golden tint now with all the lights on.

"We have to check a few things." The doctor pulls the covers down, raises Mike's left arm over the sheet, and pushes up Mike's sleeve. With the tips of his fingers, Doc feels for a vein. Watching with curiosity, Mike thinks again and for the last time about skin upon skin contact. People touching his body, him not feeling it. How he needed hands on him to survive, but it's been so long since he felt anything below the neck. Like living in a jar, cut off from human touch. A fleeting thought escapes about Jenna's fingers and how the pressure of them reached deep inside even though he couldn't feel.

"Now," Doc looks up, glasses sliding down his nose as he takes a long look at Mike then turns to Bill who nods. Doc sits at the foot of Mike's bed, his back to the camera with the angle clear to record Mike's face.

Pushing up his glasses he says, "Mike, are you here of your own free will? Answer as clearly as you can."

"Yes," Mike says to the camera, then looks at doctor, "Yes." In front of a camera, he thinks, his heart beginning to thud. Not the way I thought. Tears threaten. He swallows.

"Do you understand that you have asked me to attach an IV, a tube from this pouch," he holds up the clear, plastic pouch, "to a needle in your arm?"

"Yes," Mike says again, looking at the doctor, not the camera, his eyes level.

"This valve," he touches the bottom of the pouch, "is attached to the string, which has a handle on the end." He holds up the handle, the string draping between it and the bag. "I'm going to tie the handle around your hand and when you tug—can you tug please, move your hand for the camera?"

Mike moves his arm in the practiced motion, six inches of victory after 20 years, now used to "off" himself. Maybe that's why he'd practiced.

"Good. When you pull the string, the medicine that will stop your heart is released into your system, causing cardiac arrest. Your body will stop functioning, causing death. Do you understand, Mike?"

"My body stopped functioning long ago, Doc."

A slight chuckle, "I understand. Please answer yes or no."

"Yes, I understand ... know ... that I'll die," and his voice cracks and he's unable to contain the tears.

The doctor doesn't move other than to place his hand reassuringly on Mike's knee. In a soft voice, "Do you understand that we can call your brother and you can reconsider your decision? We can postpone or cancel. It is no trouble to me," he motions backwards, "or to Bill. You are in charge and things will happen only at your request."

In charge. Yea, I'm in charge, Mike thinks. Finally, forever. My last charge.

Getting hold of himself, sniffling, Mike says, "I'm ready, Doc. Let's do it. Can you wipe my face, please? I'm sorry."

"No trouble, no trouble," the doctor goes to the bedside table and does what Tommy did a few short hours, days, years ago. Careful to wipe under Mike's glasses, the Doc fixes them again on his face. Glasses that'll keep the wind out of his eyes when he runs.

"Did you get it all Bill?"

"Yes. All there."

"Will you check please while I set up the IV?"

Bill does as he's asked, efficient, not looking at Mike except when his eye is trained on him through the lens.

"Do you need some water? Anything to drink?" the doctor asks as he hangs the empty pouch from the pole.

Throat and lips dry, Mike remembers all the times he craved water, needed it, enjoyed its life giving force. "No ... thanks," he answers and looks to the ceiling.

Metal squeaks as Bill adjusts the tripod for a better angle. Doc goes to the desk with what looks like a shaving case. Mike hears the clink of small glass and then liquid being poured. He tries to keep his mind blank, having thought all the thoughts he could think, wondering if he forgot anything, if there is anything left to think. A sickness rises inside, one threatening to spill.

"Can you give me something, Doc ... before the real thing, I mean?"

The doctor pushes past Bill and comes to the bedside. "Bill, please, the camera." Careful to stand so Bill can see Mike's face, the doctor says, "It's only a few moments, now. Are you feeling ok?" His glasses are sliding again and he looks down his nose at Mike.

"Feeling a little sick, weird ... scared."

Patting Mike's arm, he takes the handle hanging from the string and holds it up, a question in his eyes. Mike nods, lips shaking. Doc positions the handle in his hand then wraps the string around Mike's wrist. Carefully and slowly, the needle at the end of the IV tube is inserted. He's attached. Ready to fly from this world to the next once the medicine is poured.

He almost laughs at the simplicity of it. Remembers all the schemes he and his brothers dreamed up about how he could end his own life—a rifle propped to his head, poison mixed in a drink, a stripper feeding him pills one by one—trouble was, someone had to do it. Set it up. And the guys didn't have the heart for it. Now, he's pulling a string to end his life. A thin string not much wider than the separation in his spine. Wished he'd of thought of it sooner.

"We can stop, we can wait, we can go home," Doc says. Mike doesn't say anything, so he continues. "When you pull on this," he taps the handle that is now positioned in Mike's hand, "after the medicine is poured ... can you pull for me?"

Mike tugs and the valve opens. Practice. Like on the field or the stage, when he played the leading role. Guess this is why they call it a dry run.

Nodding, the doctor turns back to him. "It's working fine. I just have to pour the liquid into the pouch, as you have asked that I do. I am here only to assist you. But I will not pour the liquid until I'm told by you, so take your time, take your time." He resets the valve then goes back to the desk to finish mixing the drugs.

Gazing at the ceiling Mike tries to see through it. Imagines the dark, cold sky. Needs to think of something warm. In his mind's eye he sees the ocean, the Jersey shore, with rolling waves on a wide beach. He'll go there, glances at his hand, with a small motion. His big accomplishment.

All the years of practice, pain, sweat, come down to this. No ball thrown perfectly to a receiver or in the strike zone. Just a tug. No more, no less. To end his life. To get to the beach. "Doc?" The doctor turns and looks. "You ready?"

CHAPTER 7

1973

You need a little bit o' soul to put you right.

The Ramones

To feel or not to feel—that's Mike's Hamlet. What he feels, he doesn't like, but it gives the doctors hope. Shooting pains at the base of the neck, cramping in his legs, a slow burn in the back and spine. As much as he wants it to stop, he prays it doesn't.

When he's not praying, he's reciting Shakespeare in his head. No longer running plays in his head. Decides to focus on what he can practice with his mind, not his body.

He knows most of Hamlet's lines 'cause he'd practice in secret in his bedroom mirror, imagining being on stage capturing everyone's attention. The soliloquy's his favorite:

"To be or not to be, that is the question." When he was younger, Mike used to drape a sheet over his shoulders and swing his arm wide when he said it, encompassing the world in one small motion.

"Whether 'tis nobler in the mind to suffer the slings and arrows of outrageous fortune, or to take arms against a sea of troubles and by opposing, end them. To die, to sleep, no more, and by a sleep to say we end the heartache, and the thousand natural shocks that flesh is heir to. 'Tis a consummation

devoutly to be wished." The words ring differently now that he's flat on his ass. Wonders if Shakespeare ever thought about the not feeling, the not being. Wonders if the small space in his spine causing the 'not feeling' will cause the 'not being.'

Loosening the ropes, he can finally bear to be awake for longer periods. When traction ended, he still had to lay flat, but no more flipping. Now they rolled him over. The first time he nearly blacked out; then he'd grit his teeth and set his jaw when they moved him. Now it's routine. Still hurts but he likes the hurt 'cause he feels it.

Tons of people visit, though none are allowed in the room. Only siblings, mom and the priest are allowed in 'cause he's "susceptible." Everyone else files past a big window to his right, where the nurses keep an eye on him from their station across the hall. Cards and letters pile on a table outside the room. Judy and Rita sort through and read to him, taping funny ones to the wall.

Visitors keep coming once word gets out he's off the ropes. From the corner of his eye, Mike sees faces file past the window gaping at the living dead. Friends, family, some unrecognizable faces, all wide-eyed taking in the gruesome details seeing him locked in here. Through the drug haze, he didn't care. When they reduced the meds, he was self conscious at first, unable to wave or nod. I'm on stage, alright. Joe tells him to ease up—that people are concerned. That he should be grateful. Grateful—a word that sticks at odd angles in his head.

Lots of classmates come—from Tremont and Washington. Morris Hospital is 40 minutes from Somers, so he appreciates the effort and time. Some bring signs and hold them on the glass—"Get well Mike" or "We love you Mike!" Others wave, girls throw kisses.

Dad doesn't show. Even drugged up Mike knew, but refused to ask. He'd see it on mom's face, her tight smile when the whole family was there but not him, her face holding back her own devils. Hell, she had to live with him.

Every day he doesn't come, a callous grows on top of the one that started when he was a kid—when he picked up a football—when a gradual shift bore down on them. Dad looked away when Mike threw the ball in a sharp spin through a tire swing. Mike would smile and look to him for approval. But Dad's cloudy eyes grew the callous; his absent eyes formed layer upon layer through the years till it was a hard nub inside.

Born Alex G. Murphy, Jr., it was Dad who nicknamed him Mike. Dad never wanted a "Junior," but mom insisted. He called him Mike playfully to annoy her and it stuck.

Dad played baseball and almost made the minor leagues. He was the first to put a baseball in Mike's hand. At the time, Mike was four or five watching Dad's strong hand roll the ball while explaining the seams and showing him how to place his fingers just so. Dad showed Joe too, but he concentrated with Mike 'cause of the talent. Mike was a natural and took to pitching instantly. Maybe it was the attention, maybe the approval in Dad's eyes that made him like it. The finer the pitching, the warmer the light.

When Mike played football, Dad didn't spend the time—seemed to work more at the hardware store where he sold paint and did odd jobs. He could build a house soup to nuts and he did all of the work around their house. Mike used to follow him, watching the way his hands knew the placement of wood, how he could measure without a tape.

It confused Mike when his grade school football team won and Dad was silent, just nodding as Mike and Joe romped and mimicked the plays and what happened. Even during baseball season he grew cooler, standoffish. The more he withdrew, the cockier Mike was about throwing the football in his face. He practiced and played to hone his skills to prove to Dad that he could play both sports and excel.

Sometimes when he was younger they'd fight. Dad yelled that football was "no good" that he would "come to no good" if he didn't quit. Those words were the seeds that grew arrogance in Mike's eyes. More discouragement meant more playing for Mike. His rebellion twisted and grew like a gnarled tree with withered limbs and craggy feet. The roots were his cleats, firmly dug in and planted on the goal line.

When he made the team at Bishop Tremont, Dad's chin went up and lids lowered, as if he couldn't look Mike straight on. Mike responded with a smirk, never looking too close at the eyes of stone—afraid of what was behind them. Whether love or hate, it could kill him.

Mike remembered the conversation at dinner when he told his folks he was transferring to Washington after the coach at Tremont benched him. They ate in the kitchen at a big oval table, the kids lining the sides, mom and Dad at either end. Joe was in college but everyone else was there, Rita working nine to five, Judy at Tremont, and Tommy in grade school.

"Well you must think you're hot stuff," Dad had said, stopping forks midway to mouths. No one wanted a show down.

"I just want to play," Mike had answered, continuing to eat—chicken and mashed potatoes—steaming hot, the way he liked.

"What about the kid who's played for three years, who won't play because of you?"

Mike glanced at mom, who didn't take sides with her eyes. "Coach said he needed me—nobody strong coming up."

Dad wiped his mouth on a cloth napkin and threw it on the table. "Might not be a good idea according to the doctor."

"Full ride to Notre Dame," Mike shrugged.

When Dad left the table, the only sound was silverware clinking. It was the last time they spoke.

⌘ ⌘ ⌘

"Got a surprise for you!" Joe's carrying a big box. Behind him, Rob Snider, Tremont's kicker, trails with a smaller box. Mike forces his eyes down to see. Eyeballs hurt from strain—the only thing he can move, the only restful place the ceiling.

The two guys bend over, their backs popping in and out of his line of sight. Lots of commotion and shuffling, some cursing. It's almost six o'clock, visiting hours.

"Gang from Tremont will be here tonight," Joe's voice is muffled. "Rob, plug this in over there—watch that," Joe points to a tall monitor that blinks and beeps. "Don't knock it over."

"What's goin' on?" Mike asks. Rob disappears and Mike hears him crawling around while Joe clears off a tray then lifts a stereo onto it. Next he places a record player on top and reaches in back to plug in the speakers that Rob is setting up on either side of the tray. Each speaker is about two feet high.

"You guys are nuts. Nurses'll kill you." Mike glances through the window. The station's empty.

"We'll see," Rob says clapping dust off his hands, smiling his baby face smile. He looks like Ben Vereen, only white.

"You're not even supposed to be in here," Mike says.

"I'm clean!" Rob raises his arms open wide.

"You know how you said you feel funny just laying here?" Joe asks, "Well, now you're the host—the life of the party," he flips through albums. Finds one. "A little music to bring some LIFE IN HERE," he circles raising the album up and down in a mummer's strut.

Mike laughs. "Got any beer?"

Joe takes the album out of its sleeve, checks the label, loads it on the player, picks up the arm and places the needle in the groove.

Deep base notes crackle and fill the room, then rhythmic clapping and voices. Grand Funk Railroad's *Loco-motion*. Joe's head nods in time while Rob adjusts the volume. Guitars kick in and music fills Mike's head, pushing the pain away with familiar tones bringing memories of good times, from before. Like a salve, the sounds wash over him.

Joe turns it up. He and Rob clap and dance the way guys do, just moving their knees up and down, singing, acting goofy. Mike pictures himself moving and clapping, knees bending in a simple motion that's impossible, that he's determined to do again once these screws are out of his back.

Mouthing the words, eyes closed, he sees his long legs sure and steady moving in time to the beat, like silk, graceful. He could see himself hamming it up like he did at weddings and parties, or the junior prom when he jumped on stage, pulled off his bowtie and twirled it while everyone cheered. Though his body is still, his mind rocks.

Joe leans over, smiling. "Havin' fun?"

"Thanks, man," Mike says.

"It's party time!" Judy comes in snapping her fingers. And with that the line dance starts. Through the window, Tony and Steve appear—basketball players at Tremont, followed by the Smith's—seven kids—so many of them, including Maryann, the girl he took to the prom, and her sister, Betty. Goofing around they wave, give him a thumbs up, then gather somewhere down the hall so the rest of the long line can pass by.

There's Tim and Pat, and Mary and Paul, couples that have been together forever. Mary looks like she's crying. Next to her is Debbie, who Rob dances out to greet 'cause they're dating. There's Penny and Sue, who's a cheerleader. Sue gave him a ride home from a party at Tremont the night before the game because she had an early curfew and he needed to sleep. Remembers telling her how he missed his friends and that he was a little nervous about the game. She said something strange that he forgot about until just now—she said she thought he was special and that playing at Washington would show everyone how brave he was.

Rita comes in and turns one of the speakers to face the hallway. The nurses don't object 'cause visitors from other rooms know Mike and they're dancing too.

So begins the tradition of music to brighten spirits and dispel heartache. Playing records is an easy way to host visitors; Mike can listen like everyone else.

Tonight, laying here, pain meds in full force, a party going on outside his room, Mike releases his mind to a place of relief. A place where the love of his friends and family lives, a beach of warm sand, the sun brightening a new day, with diamonds dancing on the reflecting waves. A beach where he doesn't struggle to move. In the years to come, he'll go there when he needs quiet, a respite, or to keep his sanity. Tonight, he goes there to dance.

CHAPTER 8

1968

Good morning starshine, the earth says hello.
You twinkle above us, we twinkle below.

Oliver

He's riding in the backseat of a station wagon, windows open, hair blowing. Dad and Joe are up front. Joe's turning the dial on the radio trying to find his station. Mom always sets it to WIP, old songs; Joe likes MMR, hard rock, The Who, Doors, stuff like that, but he can't find it so he settles for WIBG—Wibbage—a kind of bubble gum station that sells flower power decals and albums of the top ten. Mike doesn't care what's on. Just listening to the wind in his ears is enough.

Baseball mitt on the seat next to him, Mike is proud of how he used it. Pitching, he'd caught three fly balls, which is unheard of for a pitcher. Two were bunts gone bad; one just luck. Coach jumped up and down 'cause his last catch won the game. Dad's eyes were proud when Mike came off the field. Patted him on the back, said, "Good job," while Joe was all smiles replaying the catches as they walked to the car, exaggerating how quick Mike was on the mound. Joe was always proud, always there to cheer him on. Now that he's in high school and Mike is in sixth grade, they're not on the same team anymore. Fact is, Joe doesn't play at all anymore, just on the side of the house catching for Mike.

"You looked good out there, son," Dad says looking in the rearview mirror.

"Yea, thanks, Dad. Next week's the playoffs."

"I'll be there," Dad's eyes smile. Always came to Mike's baseball games. Didn't have time for football.

Last year, when Mike picked up a football, Dad backed off, had other things to do instead of going to the games or practices. When Mike asked him to throw a ball around if Joe was working or something, he would, but he'd only throw the small, white ball. Dad avoided the pigskin and said Mike should too. Now, with summer coming, it'd be smooth sailing with Dad. 'Til August when he'd put on his cleats.

Eyes squinting against the wind, Mike reviewed his pitching. Had a few strikeouts, not enough. Have to get the ball tighter inside. Couldn't wait to watch the Phillies on Saturday, watch the way the pitcher moved. After the game, he and Joe will go outside and Mike'll practice the movements, imitating what the pitcher did, down to the eyes looking out under the cap for the signal, with Joe coaching him.

He did the same with football, 'cept it's harder to imitate a quarterback—movements are bigger than a pitcher's. Had to be quick with hands and feet, stay in the pocket while finding his grip, placing his fingers just so to throw a perfect spiral. He liked the feel of a football, the shape of it, pointed on either end. He liked the way his arm felt in full throttle following through after a pass, sweeping out and down, extended, the pressure in the bones and muscles adjusting, depending on where the receiver was on the field. Magic when the ball's caught in a tight opening, connecting him and the receiver perfectly as if a string went between them.

Dad didn't understand when Mike tried to tell him how it felt different. Pitching is throwing against someone, to trick or beat the batter; quarterbacking is with someone, with a team, blockers doing their thing so he and the receivers connect. Football is all forward motion through teamwork. Couldn't help but like it. Couldn't help but like being in control of it. Quarterbacking fit his style like the football fit in his hand.

He also liked the attention football brought from his friends—the way they looked up to him. Liked the attention from girls better. They'd giggle and cover their mouths with their hands, whispering when he walked by in the hallway the day after a game. At first, he never said anything, just thought it was cool. Made him walk a little taller. Then, he'd catch the eye of the prettiest girl and make a joke, watch her smile widen, the other girls looking on.

Glibby gloop glibby, nibby nabby noopy, la la la lo lo …. Crazy lyrics from the radio catch his attention. "Hey, Joe, turn this up," he says.

Dad glances in the rearview as Joe makes it louder. Tic toc noises turn into musical verses. *Can you hear me e e e e … lovin' a song, laughin' a song, singin' a song.* Joe turns and smiles.

Face in the wind, Mike knows he's safe, that his family, Dad, mom, Joe, are the springboard of his life. *Sing the song, song the sing, song song song si-ing sing sing si-ing song.* He feels possibilities opening like a flower, dewy, young, ready for the sun's rays to shine down on him, give him the spotlight.

Almost bursting inside, he's jittery, anxious to get home, eat, go outside and play. Hoped Joe didn't have a lot of homework. *Yea-a, you can sing, sing a song, sing a song…. Sing!*

CHAPTER 9

1974

Dreams in my head all turning dark and useless.
Grand Funk Railroad

Little things he missed most: diners, shooting hoops, sitting on the lawn, driving, showering, picking eye sleep, scratching a good itch.

Sitting on the front porch with leaves raining yellow and gold matching the scarf tucked into his coat, Mike's mind is wandering to things he did so recently it felt like yesterday. He thinks of the diner, Somers South, where everyone goes after dances. Where at 2 a.m., sitting in a booth with the guys holding court, girls fluttering like moths, he'd order a cheesesteak with onions and mushrooms. Can almost taste the sweet, invisible cheese all mixed in with the steak, the hard roll satisfying to the bite. Sometimes a chocolate shake to wash it down. Just hanging out, waitresses yelling orders, clanging dishes and silverware, cars outside trolling. No reason to go there now; can't hold a fork. And the eye sleep, well now he has to wait for mom or the nurse to clean it out.

Lots of things to get used to, like the wheelchair. Has to stay leaned back in it 'cause he can't sit straight. Tilts over. He's workin' on that though, to train the muscles in his back to hold him steady.

When he first got home, his nurse, a big guy with a trim Afro and gentle hands, lifted him into the chair. Mike made him sit it upright, the guy arguing, shaking his head saying it wouldn't work. Mike insisted. While the guy was changing the sheets, Mike started leaning forward, his body just goin'. He couldn't stop the motion, the floor coming up at him with no way to break his fall. Like on the Trabant, a ride on Wildwood's boardwalk that flung him close to the ground, his stomach lurched. Unlike the boardwalk, the horror was real and he couldn't protect his face. The nurse caught him six inches from the floor, his strong arms lifting, preventing a broken nose and then some. The whole scene opened a humble pocket inside of Mike, where he now hides his impotence, even from himself.

Leaning back in the chair outside his room, the addition Dad built while he was in rehab, his eyes look across the lawn to the quiet street. There's never traffic on it, just who lived in the neighborhood. This being a weekday, all the Dad's are at work, like his, and mom's are cleaning and shopping. Kids are at school. His eyes drop to legs that still have weight on them, though they're thinner than before. Makes the therapists work them hard for when he can walk again. Has to walk. Has to get out of the chair. Thinks hard about it. Talks to Joe every day when he works his legs some more. Joe's at La Salle College in the city, but lives home now to help mom.

In the late afternoon, after Joe and Mike have a bite to eat, the music's turned on and, instead of throwing a football, he and Joe throw thoughts and ideas around on how to end the madness. In his rectangular room with a wall unit on one side and windows on the other, he and Joe plan and work to get his feet flat again. Trouble is, they droop a little more each day. While Joe pushes and pulls, Mike turns his head to the twenty feet of space from his bed to the windows, space for friends to gather or dance if there's a party. Tries to ignore what Joe's doing and not see the mutilation happening little by little. Without feet standing flat, he can't run no matter what happens in his spine. Sometimes when the pain's biting into his back like a snake with its teeth sunk in, he tries to send the pain to his feet to get them to move. Never works. He doesn't understand how pain signals can jump the small break and not the good signals.

A train whistle low and faraway reminds him of a dream he had last night. Except in last night's dream, the train's horn was right on his back.

He dreamt that he and Joe were walking along train tracks in a desert, the sand hot and dry. A horn blows loud behind them and they don't have a chance to look back, just know they have to run. Mike's pushing Joe yelling, "This way! This way!" They are safely off the tracks still running when the train passes them and speeds crazily into a sharp bend ahead. Mike knows it's going too fast. The train skids and falls on its side and he and Joe watch, thinking they're safe, out of harm's way. But it's sliding toward them and the black top of a blue car comes right at them and Mike knows they'll die. The train car hits them but Mike doesn't feel the pain. He lands in a blue, watery world, floating on his back, submerged, small bubbles coming from his mouth. There's no sound but the fullness of water in his ears. He sucks in salty water and when his lungs are full, it doesn't hurt, just stops the bubbles. He curls into a ball and sees his feet. They're strong and flat. All is quiet except for his heartbeat, like in the huddle. But he's dead, and it feels cozy and warm and he knows he has to wake up or stay there. It's quiet, serene, like a womb. And he hears mom's voice, "Mike, Mike," and he's glad to hear it and he opens his eyes to the sun shining in his room. Another day to try. He was glad to see mom, knowing it wasn't time yet to float into the silent world. He still wanted to hear music and dance. Someday, he would dance.

A breeze blows more leaves from the trees and they're raining down now, still fresh and dewy, not crinkly yet. Wishes he could pile in them. The smell in the air is football. Makes him crazy. Makes him feel like his feet, dying a little bit at a time.

CHAPTER 10

1983

I wish I had a river I could skate away on.

Joni Mitchell

The first 10 years were shock and hope. Shock that it had happened; hope that it would end. Through it all, Mike rode a wave of stardom from his bed in Somers. Activity prevailed in his room. Reporters kept coming — *Somers Courier Times, The Evening Bulletin*—all the attention keeping the pain at bay. Mike always greeted visitors with a smile, though hours before he sweated through physical therapy, pushing the therapists to keep him in athletic shape.

In rehab in 1974, Mike spent the winter learning to manage the pain and to move his arms. Designated a quadriplegic by the location of where his spine snapped, any movement below the neck brought magic, awe—the kind that connected people. With his determined focus and the iron will of an athlete, Mike became living proof of the triumph of the human spirit. With each millimeter of movement, the doctors' collective jaws dropped and the nurses smiled. Family and friends encouraged, and Mike, in a bed of ropes and pulleys, grew seeds of hope to conquer this mishap—a mistake, a bad choice, a goof.

Looking out from eyes still dusted with adolescent arrogance, Mike saw the stunned surprise when a bicep raised his arm off the bed. Sparkling eyes cheered him on just like when he played. Visitors, fans, friends participated in his success, made him want to practice. So he did, day after day, pushing through pain and sweat till he could raise both arms giving him some control—to push the button on his wheelchair and to dial a phone. His body still looked like something back then, before muscles collapsed and dissolved leaving him a stick figure with his family as arms and legs.

"I made the chicken like you wanted," mom says coming into his room balancing a tray. Before closing the door behind her, the noise from Dad's TV in the den fills his room with sounds of crowds and cheering. Mike is watching the game too—the Phillies in Atlanta. The smell of roasted chicken fills him with memories of childhood—of coming in from practicing in the yard with Joe, all boy sweat, washing hands in the powder room and then chowin' down.

Mom pulls away his "desk" (the phone tray covered with papers) and pushes the food tray over the bed. "Want the TV on or off?" she asks.

"Aw, they're losing. Turn it off." He thought the Phil's might win the series again this year, like they did in '80. Lots of excitement here during that series, with crowds of friends and parties in his room while watching the games. A picture of Eileen comes to his mind, a girl he dated when the Phil's won the championship.

Eileen was a friend of a friend, that kind of thing. He met her when he was out with Joe at the Willows, a local bar where kids just back from college hang out. It's dark and friendly and Mike was a regular there for a while. He used to sit at a table in the corner where he could see everything—where the chair wasn't too obvious.

People always came up to him to talk about the articles in the papers about him, his charity work or a sporting event. Local fame. On the night he'd met Eileen, he looked good in a pullover sweater, his shirt collar starchy on his neck. She came over to the table with a couple of people and sat next to him. While drawing circles with her finger in the wet from her beer glass, she'd told him she saw the accident; that she was a junior at Washington when it happened. Said she'd read about him a lot over the years, but not knowing him, felt funny about visiting. Glad she ran into him here.

Mike's face flushed and he was glad for the dim lights. She'd seen him on the field, when he was tall, in full regalia. She'd seen photos in newspapers of him in this chair and now she talked to him like a regular guy, still wanting to get to know him. And she touched her hand to his arm saying how sorry she was, but smiling coyly. Through the wool sweater, he had felt the tug of her fingers and was instantly turned on, which these days meant signals in his head went haywire with nowhere to go but crazy.

Petite, with curly brown hair, she was cute. Built like a gymnast, her stature came in handy in later weeks maneuvering in his bed. Though he couldn't do much, she did plenty.

But the physical connection wasn't enough. Wasn't his type. Even though he's a quad in a chair, he still has a type. With Eileen, their actions were hungry, animal, action in his head on full tilt. When his face was buried in one crease of her body or another, the notes played but he couldn't hear the music. After a while, he was empty, like the tin man, a big barrel of nothing, with metal skin that couldn't feel. His mind would sit back and wait for it to be over. But it was him being grateful that really turned his stomach, and why he broke it off after a few months.

Mom turns off the TV and baseball sounds are replaced with rain pounding on the roof. It's one of those downpours where the sky opens up and everything falls in a sheet. He sees it through the wall of windows to his right, windows that frame the trees, street, and on nice days, folks walking by. Many times, someone just knocks, drops in to say hi, then another and another, and soon fifteen people are in the room.

Mom sits on the stool and picks up the utensils to cut his food. Mike always tells her to cut the food in the kitchen where it's easier, but she says no. It's his meal and he should eat like an adult, not a baby who can't cut.

Smiling, she lifts a forkful of chicken and mashed potatoes, with an extra dip in gravy, to his mouth. The bib's in place—he calls it a bib. She says apron 'cause it's starched white linen like a chef's but short, tied around his neck. For every meal, a clean bib. Sometimes dried in the sun with a fresh air smell, always ironed. She did everything to make him feel like a regular person.

"Mmmm, it's good," he says after chewing the first bite.

"Your favorite!" Her voice is soft. His face is thin like hers but she's redhead Irish with freckles and he's black Irish—dark hair and eyes, like his father. His beard is tight around his face so they don't have to shave him every day. One of his sisters trims it once a week or whenever. Mom doesn't like it—thinks it makes him look sunken. Every morning, she asks if he wants a shave.

"Are the posters ready?" he asks.

"All set. Your sister has them in her car."

There's a fundraiser Friday night for Step by Step, a non-profit Mike started about six years ago. The money went to local kids in wheelchairs who needed therapy or equipment. Sometimes donations went to Special Olympics, or to science to find a cure. Mike had great success hosting events 'cause of his popularity as a local celebrity. Sports writers loved him. And, for a couple of years, he coached little league and developed a few kids into great athletes.

Once, he'd organized a basketball game between some of the Phillies and Tremont's football team. His events always drew a crowd. Early on, Mike realized that the strength of his magnetism had nothing to do with his body. People were attracted to the pull of his eyes. He'd joke, tell stories, and make people comfortable by holding their attention with a look or with the control in his voice. And they always came back.

Including the gang of people who came to a special fundraiser about four years ago for research into this "walking machine" a guy named Herb Blascomb invented. Herb built an experimental device aimed to train muscles to walk again through movement and practice. Mike was all for the practicing idea, lived it, knowing practice brought results.

Now, when thinking about the contraption, he could laugh or cry, depending on his mood. Reminiscing with his brothers, he'd laugh and make fun. But by himself, all he remembers is the terror and desperation that made him want to try it.

Blascomb had designed a metal frame to fit around his body, operated by electronic signals that moved the metal. The best it did was stand him up.

The hustle around the project was astronomical. Blascomb met with Mike and his brothers many nights and weekends, talking, planning. Mike thought the metal would make him look more like a freak than he already did. But with encouragement, he'd agreed 'cause it was stepping toward hope. Moving in a positive direction, thinking forward not back. Also, it kept away the dark thoughts that flashed in his mind—thoughts that if shown daylight would grow and spread like cancer.

When Herb and his assistant, a short man with a permanent smile, wheeled in the machine in a big, black trunk, Mike's family was assembled—four siblings and mom—to see if it would work.

The girls moved things out of the way, while the men clamped the metal around him. It clanged and scraped and Mike tried not to look, feeling like he was in the circus prepping for a grotesque act. But with his family around and all the activity, hope seeded in the back of his mind while he stared at the ceiling and prayed.

When wires were connected and ready, the guys lifted him into a sitting position with his legs hanging over the side. Now he could see the extent of his deformity—flaccid feet stuck in metal shoes attached to silver calves. Tin knees, braced thighs. He sat in curved metal around his hips, rounded like a bowl to a waistband of steel. Two wide plates attached to the waistband— one covering his chest, the other his back. Arms were stuck in metal sleeves. Luckily, he had enough nerve endings from his neck to his shoulders to hold his own head. God had left some connections intact, the ones that helped him move his arms. It was a blessing and a curse having those nerve endings 'cause they could also signal a cramp or send hot needles of stinging pain.

"Okay, Mike, I'm going to move your leg now," Herb said. Mike was glad his dead fish feet were covered with metal. Now they looked like something.

Herb's face was sweating, though his smile was broad. He was leaning over looking at the knee coverings, his hand on a valve. His gray suit was wilting.

Mike eyeballed Joe, whose smile looked a little like the assistant's—it didn't reach his eyes. One thing, he was sitting up within the brace, not leaning on anything for the first time in six years. He wished he could feel relief like when you move a sore muscle, but there was only blankness below his neck, except for a kind of settling in his stomach. No pain today, which was odd.

Mom stood in front of the window facing Mike clasping hands to her mouth, maybe remembering another first step a long time ago. Tommy came close to the bed and stood next to Herb. They were positioned like characters in a science fiction film—all waiting to see the new creation.

There was a buzzing sound and his leg moved up, from the knee, without help from Joe or Tommy or anybody else. Laughter broke the tension and Mike tried not to cry. Another buzz and the leg went down.

"Heh?" Herb nodded smiling at Mike, like "See?"

"Let's go!" Mike said with enthusiasm, though his voice cracked.

Joe and Tommy moved on either side and braced under his arms. A whirring sound lifted him off the bed—his rear end was off the bed! Up he went, taller than Joe, taller than Tommy, looking at his mom, tears in her eyes.

His face was excitement, surprise. Seeing the room from six feet three inches was thrilling. Looking down to his mom was life.

"Wow!" Joe didn't let go but he stepped back to look up. "Haven't seen this angle in a while," he said in a whisper.

The girls came closer, their bright eyes shining.

"Whoo hoo!" Tommy said. He had always looked up to his brother—literally, growing up watching Mike and Joe play sports, watching Mike at his games. Now he was looking across, almost eye level, though not quite. "You're the man," he said in a low voice only Mike could hear.

Mike glanced over and smiled. Feeling a surge in his body that must have been adrenalin, one that made him want to jump up and down, he said to Herb, "Make me walk."

After adjusting wires and playing with the machine, a button was pushed and his right leg slid forward. Mom gasped, otherwise it was quiet, like the room was holding its breath. More whirring and his left leg slid to meet the right.

"Again!" Herb shouted to his assistant who now pressed the buttons.

His legs slid again and Mike felt like he was on a thin sheet of ice that could break at any moment. There was no looking down; he kept his eyes straight ahead.

"Let go of him," Herb said.

Joe stepped back smiling; Tommy hesitated then let go but didn't move away. Without support, Mike toppled toward Tommy. One moment on top of the world, held aloft by machinery and magic, standing, actually standing, and the next he was the Leaning Tower of Pisa. No balance. Unable to feel nuances that lived somewhere in the ears to hold himself up. Guess Herb tried the machine with people who could balance.

Tommy grabbed under his arm and Joe came back to his post on the other side. Mom shook her head and cried into her hands, the girls converging murmuring hope. Mom looked up, eyes wet, and the three women faced Mike and his brothers. Rita's open, Irish face hopeful, Judy's narrow face somber. There they stood—men of the family facing the women. Three to three. The one missing in the den.

"Let's try again," Mike said knowing it wouldn't work, wasn't going to work. But he had to keep his chin up for the family.

"Stay with him for one more cycle." Herb said. Leaning down, he fiddled with the knobs mumbling to his assistant. "Here we go!"

Again, one foot slid, then the other—another step closer to mom—and the door. Mike imagined sliding right out the door, a head on stilts, a monster machine sliding down the street scaring all the kids.

"What do you think, Mike?" Joe asked in a way that gave the answer.

Glancing at mom, whose hands were clasped under her chin white-knuckled with nerves (or maybe she was praying), Mike didn't want to diminish the remnant of hope in her eyes. He stood for one more minute knowing this may be the last, the very last time he was at full height. He knew that expectations would be dashed and disappointment would rule. Having no other choice he said, "I'm tired."

They laid him down on the bed and disassembled the metal, all the while talking and busy as if they would try again, that with a few adjustments it would work, knowing it was a show. That the fixing had to be done in his spine, not the machine.

Herb and his assistant packed up and said a hearty goodbye with a promise to call in a week or two after working things out. They turned and wheeled the black trunk out the door, taking Mike's hope with them. They never saw Herb again.

⌘　⌘　⌘

"How many people are you expecting?" Mom's almost finished feeding him, scraping the last of the potatoes onto the fork.

"About 150. We got the same DJ as before. Good dancing last time," Mike says.

Mom never went to the fundraisers. She wanted it to be like a dance for him where parents didn't go. Mike always asked her to come, but liked that she didn't. It made him feel like he's in charge—nobody over him.

After the last dance, about three months ago, he met this girl, Marjorie. She was from Washington High, but he never saw her before, not really having time to get to know anyone there. She worked at IVB—Industrial Valley Bank in Pottsville, about 20 minutes from Somers. Cute figure, long curly hair. She came over a few times after the dance—he liked her button nose and pretty hands. They kissed a little but that was that. Had a bad spell of pain and some fever so he never followed up, though Tommy told him to 'cause she kept calling. But with most girls it ended the same—lots of kissing but he couldn't take them to dinner or a concert, support them, or unbutton their blouses.

And those nerves God left connected, well sometimes those nerves worked where it counted and the natural urges of a 27 year old lodged in his mind and he couldn't push them out. Those were tough days, weeks sometimes.

"Want the game back on?" mom asks.

Mike shakes his head.

"I'll bring dessert in a bit." She opens door and he hears the game still on in the den. She closes the door behind her.

In the quiet, his mouth sets in a grim line. The body is quiet today too—no cramps or burning. Turning, he looks at the rain washing down the panes of glass and he thinks of waterfalls in a tropical park. Pictures himself standing under it, water hitting his face and chest, looking up to the sky, trees jutting from rocks rising high above him, legs under him strong against the pounding water, strong enough to withstand its massage, feet on rocks under clear water that sparkles white.

When he daydreamed, he always tried to picture the same girl with him. A girl he named Grace that came to him in night dreams. She was a regular who lived inside his head like a night fairy, her magic working only in the dark. He tried to bring her into daylight today by thinking of her under the falls with him, untying her bikini top and going where a man wants to go. But she stayed tucked inside. Knowing mom's coming back with dessert, all he sees is the teeming water on the window.

Turning to the ceiling, a fly walks upside down, hanging by its sticky feet. The fan, installed about five years ago, is off. Mom wanted a white fan. Mike argued for brown or wicker or something his eyes could fall into. It's white.

Glancing at the phone table, it's too far to reach. Did I order enough food? Ask Judy to call about the beer and set ups. I'll go over the music with Joe tomorrow. Don't want to play the same songs, even though last time was great. Just something different. He keeps lists in his mind, memorizing what has to be done then checking things off with an imaginary pen.

The more on his mind, the better. Keeping ghosts away is a full time job. Most days he has help—therapy, the nurse that still comes to wash him, get him ready for the day. Even meals with company helps. His family treats him like he's normal and they never let on if they're tired of taking care of him. This keeps him alive, which is good. But it also keeps him optimistic, which is bad. Sometimes he just wants to fade away. Sometimes he wishes he could take a pill, feed himself death. Hell, he's already half dead.

CHAPTER 11

1984

Give me a ticket for an airplane. I ain't got time to take no fast train.

Joe Cocker

"He can't throw! When are they going to jettison this guy?" Tommy yells at the TV. The Eagles are playing Dallas—a huge rivalry, and they're losing. Tommy's a guy that puts his heart and soul into watching sports. Jumps out of his seat on good and bad plays. A big guy, he takes up space. He has long legs but they're not lean like Mike's were; they're thick, muscular, and his torso and arms are filled with muscles too. A football player's body, though he never played. With a loss of four on third down with three minutes to go, he's standing, a beer in one hand, a fist in the other.

"He's doin' alright," Mike says. Jaworski has been the quarterback for the Eagles for a few years now. Mike likes him. Likes how he handles the ball in a sturdy kind of way. Confident but not cocky.

Two guys are over to watch the game—regulars—Hank and George (friends of Joe's) and Mike and his brothers. A typical football season Sunday. Mike's in bed; everyone else sits to his right. Joe's on a stool next to him, Tommy's in an armchair dragged in from the den, George is on a dining room chair and Hank on a folding lounge chair brought in from the porch. Keeping the room free of dust is mom's mission, so furniture is kept to a minimum. All chairs except the stool will go back to their places when the guys leave. A cot against the wall is for bad nights when Mike's sick or otherwise needs someone nearby. Sometimes Rita falls asleep there reading a book or watching TV. Mike doesn't mind.

"Whoo hoo!" Tommy jumps up pumping his arm. A field goal ties the game.

Watching Tommy's brisk, guy movements makes Mike itch to play, to move. The strong body moving so easily brings memories to Mike that seem impossible—memories of knees that bent without thought or effort. The wasted twigs barely lumping the covers seem surreal, even after all this time. As if he's an actor playing a part that someday will reveal its purpose; that someday will end when the scene ends.

Sometimes Mike imagines the working parts under everyone else's skin and pictures them in his own body, hoping they'll materialize. One minute Tommy's sipping a beer, the next he's airborne, arm up in happiness or disgust, depending on which team just made the play.

Is it a wish that moves muscles? Mike wished and wished. Pushing thoughts down, he swallows them—good thoughts, thoughts of walking, running, moving—positive thoughts. Memorizing Tommy's motions like he did the pitcher's when he was a kid, he pictures those motions going down his throat and sticking somewhere to glue highways back together. With so much thought in his head, so much will, he should be filled to tipping, with all the broken spaces sealed and working.

But every day his body mocks him, sitting so still with all the movement in his head. It's crazy that his curved in feet don't straighten to hold his weight so he can shift from one leg to the other. It's their job, their duty. Otherwise, why have them?

Sometimes he thinks about cutting off his legs. Then it'd be easier for mom to move him. Now, even though he's skin and bones, it's an effort for anyone to get him in the wheelchair, except for Tommy, who simply lifts him like an infant and places him wherever—in the van, in bed, in an armchair. Mike enjoys the feel of Tommy's strong arms under him, though he can't really feel them. He imagines what they're like through the enormous act Tommy performs as if it's nothing to lift 6'3" and 157 pounds of dangling limbs.

Wishes he could lift a finger. Not even an ounce of pressure is needed for that. In empty hours between visitors and a meal, he tries. Wills a finger to move. When it doesn't, he exercises, lifting one arm then the other— about 6" of movement that he's worked on through the years. Like a baby's first step, people clapped in wonder that he could move at all, which led to hope that he could do more. But all he could do is that small movement. To dial the push button phone, mom or the nurse wrap an elastic band around his hand with a pawn shaped gadget attached. Then they place an earpiece on so his calls are private. Sometimes they forget the earpiece and he uses the speakerphone, which he doesn't like 'cause he's not sure when Dad's in the den *not* watching TV.

They keep the door to his room closed at all times, except when Dad's at work. Then, after breakfast, mom leaves the door open and he can hear her singing to the radio while doing her chores. She listens to big band type music, Sinatra and such, on "her station," WIP. When she's upstairs, her voice fades but he can hear her moving from room to room. He tries to picture where she is from the sounds, in rooms he hasn't entered since the accident. He prefers to keep his paralyzed self away from the rooms where he ran and played. Wants the energy of real life memories separate from his confined life. Keeps that within the four walls of this room.

Though his room is sterile, it has a friendly feel. It's painted white with a wall unit to his left next to the den door. The stereo, albums, tapes, and photos fill the shelves. Cabinets below hold clothes, medicine, papers and stuff. Sometimes Joe tacks up a poster on the wall near the TV, like when the Phil's won the series, or from a concert. But Mike always asks one of his sisters to take it down. It makes him feel empty or like a teenager, like seeing what he's missing smack in the face.

"Yea!" The room erupts. An interception and the Eagles score with only 10 seconds to go, securing the win.

The guys slap hands and Mike smiles, raising his arm in victory—his flag of triumph. Great to beat Dallas. The only thing better is beating the Giants bad. Mike's grateful, yea grateful, for the company, to be with guys who don't pity him. But sometimes, only sometimes, it hurts to watch a game.

"Pizza!" Joe says. "Anything special?" He looks at Mike.

"The usual," Mike says meaning nothing on it. Cheese is enough. Joe leaves with his friends, everyone knowing they won't be back to eat the pie; Mike never eats in front of anyone but family.

Mom joins them later as they recap the game. She sits on the lounge chair with her feet up, listening but not really caring about what's said, nodding, chewing her slice. Mike wonders but doesn't ask what Dad's eating for dinner.

"I've been thinking about something," Mike says between bites of the slice Joe holds for him. The crust is soft the way Mike likes, with the cheese a little well done. Easier to bite.

"What else is new?" Joe smiles.

The room's quiet, TV's off, just the four of them, steaming pizza on the tray. The lid's closed but its seductive smell is all over the room.

"I watched this show yesterday—a documentary 'bout a guy named Jack Traynor."

"The running back?" Tommy asks. He's sitting on the end of the bed close to the pizza.

"No, no. This guy, Traynor, was paralyzed in World War I." Glancing at mom, she's chewing slowly, listening at full attention now. "He went to Lourdes ... you know ... in France ... where the Blessed Mother appeared ...." The room is silent. "Where she appeared to Bernadette." Mike looks at Joe whose eyes hold back waiting to hear what Mike has to say. "The guy gets there, goes in the water, and comes out walking."

Measured glances pass between brothers and mom highlighting the pause in the room, as if the steam froze for a second, as if everything froze.

"Mike," Joe starts using his calm down voice that Mike remembers from long ago when they were kids. His logical voice.

"Can we just talk about it?" Mike's voice is impatient.

"I didn't say anything," Joe says. "I just want to ..."

"Boys," mom speaks up. Joe looks at her but she doesn't look back. Her eyes are on Mike. "Let him explain," she says.

"Mom, I know I don't go to Church, that I stopped going ..." he tilts his head in a shrug. "But when I saw this show, it got me thinking."

"So, what's the deal? Where is it and all?" Tommy asks, still eating the pie. He keeps his eyes on Mike too.

"It's in France, don't know exactly where. Need some help with the details." Lifts his arms. Mike glances at Joe, whose arms are crossed and he's looking down as if already thinking of the miles they'd have to travel and the medical issues and cost. "I know it ... won't be easy ... for you guys ... you'd have to take me. Can we just look into it? See what it'll take to get there?"

Joe shakes his head but doesn't say anything.

"I gotta try. Gotta get out of this bed." Mike emphasizes to Joe. "Gotta get out of this bed, Joe," his voice cracks.

Mom stands and comes to the bed. "Of course we'll help. I'll go with you to the library." She touches his arm and he can almost feel the warmth of her fingers on his skin through her eyes.

"I'm in," Tommy says reaching for another slice. Joe gives him a look. "So, this guy walked again?"

"Let's not get too far ahead of ourselves," Joe pats the air.

Tommy shrugs.

"Let's take this one step at a time," Joe says looking at Mike.

"That's right," mom says, "one step at a time." And her eyes are like stars.

CHAPTER 12

For here am I sitting in a tin can, far above the world.

David Bowie

Flying's magic. On the top deck of a Pan Am Boeing 747, Mike's attention is split between the majestic clouds over the Atlantic and the poker game his brothers play at a table next to him in the center of the first class lounge. Only eight seats up here, two rows of two on each side lining the aisle like a movie theater. Mike and his brothers are the only passengers up top. Spiral steps behind the cockpit lead down to where other first class passengers sit.

The church raised money for the tickets. When Tommy found out about a top level, he insisted they sit behind the pilots flying the mighty bus. He had carried Mike up the narrow stairs like a baby, his strong legs pumping without effort. Mike was in the window seat leaning back, even during takeoff. Tommy sat next to him, Joe across the aisle until after dinner when the card game began.

The stewardess, blond hair in a tight knot, treats him like a regular passenger, except she has to place the straw in his mouth to drink, which he lets her do since his brothers are playing cards. When she offers, she leans over smiling, a dimple creasing her cheek and her blouse opening to a small darkness.

Reminds him of Inger Stevens, who played the Farmer's Daughter on TV years back. In black and white. Looks nicer in color.

Up here in the sky, he's held in motion, going forward in time with others, keeping up with them, not needing a push or watching as they move ahead of him, away from his chair. Up here, people restrained their movements like on a Ferris wheel, not wanting to rock the boat.

"Wanna play?" Tommy asks after another round of beating Joe at Black Jack.

Mike shakes his head, preferring to look out the window at the changing colors of twilight. Blues are running into purples and gray. Hearing the roar of the engines and feeling the lift on takeoff, Mike wants to fly forever, into the stars where the magic lived. Sensations of power fill his head after being stationary for so long, moving only with someone else's help. Now, he's sitting just like the other passengers while the engines propel them across the ocean.

Looking out, a few stars hang in the sky where they always are, showing their light only in the dark. Turning his head to look out the window slightly behind him, he sees the angle of the long wing stretching out from the body of plane. The tip seems so far away, as if it has nothing to do with him, yet without it and its red light blinking steadily like a lighthouse, he'd be tumbling through space. He imagines the wing on the other side, the matching twin. Between their wide, immobile expanse, tons of weight balance in their arms. Mike feels safe in their embrace. His mind sits with the thought that without bending or moving, wings carry.

When night comes somewhere over Greenland, they settle in to sleep. Joe puts eye shades on, says good night. Tommy gets another drink.

"She's cute, eh?" he says after the stewardess gives him peanuts and a beer. His eyes follow her.

"Looks like Inger Stevens," Mike says.

"Inga who?"

Mike chuckles, "An actress who used to be on TV. A farmer's daughter." Tom gives him a look. "Before you were born. Hey, what were you and her talking about before? Saw you over by the pantry." Both Mike and Tommy watch as she opens the cockpit door, leans in to say something, then closes the door and begins cleaning up the station.

"Oh, about art and stuff."

Mike frowns looking at Tommy, who smiles back throwing nuts in his mouth as if he talks about art every day.

"She's into painters—not the kind that paint houses, the French guys—Monet? Renoir. Said a few other names. I dunno. Says she bids trips to France so she can visit the museums."

"Doesn't look like an artist," Mike says. Her small hands are all business, cleaning up, putting things away. Right now she's rolling up napkins and tying them with a bow while she watches coffee drip into a pot.

Reminds Mike of Judy when she stops in his room on her way out for a date. She's all dressed and pretty and drops her jewelry on his tray as she does last minute stuff while talking to him. She chats as she checks her make-up, telling him where she's going and with who. Listening, he watches as she picks up tiny earrings, posts she calls them, finds the hole in her ear and attaches the small clip in the back. Precise finger movements done without a thought. Without even looking in a mirror. Using pressure and touch to put the earring in place.

"Did you hear me?" Tommy asks.

"What?"

"She said those guys, the painters, all had difficult lives," Tommy continues.

"Hmm." Mike's not really listening.

"Hardships. Hanging out drinking. Not really working, just painting. Screwed up love lives."

"Sounds like me," Mike mumbles, "except without the paint." They both laugh.

"Get some sleep," Tommy says pulling up Mike's blanket then his own. Leaves the beer on the tray and settles in.

Lights are dim in the cabin. Mike takes a long look at the stewardess then turns his eyes to the window. Stars are full out now, tiny lights dotting the vast sky. He's among them, moving through them as they spin their tales and stretch their arms wide in the curve of the night sky. He thinks about when night turns to day and the stars disappear into their secret wombs. He wonders where they go when the morning light comes, knowing their light's still there, just blanked out by the sun. Wants to take some of that light with him. Offer it to the Madonna, who he hopes will be there in her secret place, watching the hoards of hopefuls traipse past the grotto. Starlight like in Judy's fingers. What used to live in his head. He wants it there again. Hopes the tendril of a star will reach down when the water touches his back like it did for Jack Traynor, or Bernadette, who saw starlight in the rocks so long ago.

⌘　⌘　⌘

Crackling overhead, a click and the pilot's voice, "Ah, this is your Captain, Al Stella ... we're beginning our approach into Lourdes Ossun Airport ...." Mike glances at his brothers beginning to stir under their blankets. "We'll be on the ground at approximately 7:04 a.m. local time ..." the Captain continues as the stewardess appears at the top of the stairs with a tray of white washcloths rolled like diplomas. There's steam coming from them. Opening the shuttered windows, she brings in daylight.

"Good morning," she says seeing Mike awake.

"Hi." She looks the same as last night, fresh, crisp.

She holds up the tray. "May I?" she smiles. He nods. Placing the tray on the table, she reaches across Tommy who's still flat out, lifts Mike's seat a little, removes his glasses, takes a washcloth and wipes gently from his hairline to his chin. The hot cloth is soothing, her fingers beneath it welcome. When she's finished, she opens his window shade, then the one behind him.

"Can you wake my brother?" he nods to Tommy. Inger shakes Tommy's shoulder. He emerges from under the blanket, looks up at her and smiles a cheesy smile. Mike rolls his eyes.

A while later, they're awake and washed and hot breakfast is served. Mike's not hungry, so he just eats the toast.

"Big day ahead of us," Joe smiles looking over. Mike catches his eye behind Tommy's back, who's leaning forward finishing his eggs.

Speakers crackle. "Ahhh, this is the Captain again. I want to point out that the mountains on the left side of the plane are the Pyrenées, and we have Spain to our right."

The mountains are lush green at the base, rising to rock, formidable, years strong.

"Please keep your seatbelts fastened ..."

Mike thinks of the water running between the rocks and hopes it will fill his spine so he can stand strong.

"We expect a smooth landing in approximately 30 minutes."

Water to mend the tear so his legs move in rhythm to his heart.

"Thank you for flying Pan Am."

A spark to move his limbs.

"We hope you enjoyed your flight."

He thinks of the stars.

"Welcome to France."

CHAPTER 13

On the terrace of their room in the Hotel de la Fleur, Mike stares at the mountains. Unlike the majesty of the Alps, which Mike has seen only in pictures, the Pyrenées hold a certain confidence in their containment of a sacred place. There's energy in the air, a sweetness, magnitude, that Mike tries to absorb.

These mountains cushion pain. They take in sadness and return renewed air to the grotto and surrounding areas with a muted hope—a whisper that lodges in people's souls to carry them through life. Mike hoped to hear the whisper.

Breathing in the refreshing air, Mike tries to ignore the stinging in his shoulders. The trip had been arduous, with all of the transfers, papers and lines. He had practiced building stamina for the trip by staying awake in a sitting position for longer and longer periods, and forcing himself to sit in the wheelchair rather than the bed, toughing out cramps. It's a good thing too 'cause Tommy, who had bounded up the spiral stairs in the plane holding Mike in his arms, had a hard time getting him back down. Mike's "height" made it difficult to maneuver the narrow steps. Joe had to stand in front, coaching Tommy step by step as Tommy tried not to bang Mike's feet. It was a comedy act really, the three of them tired and punchy. Mike decided to crack jokes to lighten Tom's load, and all three of them and Inger laughed their way off the plane. Guess take off is easier than landing.

From plane to taxi to hotel, he was shuffled, carried, lifted, belted and fed. Though he had slept some over the ocean, he was glad to have "trained" and prided himself on his athletic ability and strength to withstand physical strain. Enthusiasm kept him agile on the field; endurance would get him through France.

Mike could hear the soft snores of his exhausted brothers coming through the open door behind him. White, sheer curtains waved in and out of the door in the breeze. After arriving this morning, Joe and Tommy wanted Mike to sleep but he was too wound up. So they unpacked and said they'd take a short nap before going to the sanctuaries. Mike asked to sit on the terrace while they slept. Wanted to take in the sights and sounds of a foreign country.

Nature is what greeted him. Mountains, trees, a river. Three floors below, a path from the hotel crossed a small bridge leading to the rocks. The hotel has an elevator to the path, making it an easy trip to the grotto. The murmured conversations of people crossing the bridge soothe Mike. He sees some people walking across, others being pushed in wheelchairs. He can't see past the curve.

Pent up inside, he's anxious to get there. Possibility beats a steady rhythm in his heart. Watching people cross the path, he wonders if they've been here before and are back for a second try. Wishes them the best but hopes they don't win the lotto before he gets there. Odds would drop.

Still can't believe he's here—for two reasons. One is that Joe finally gave in to the idea, and two, that he's sitting in a wheelchair on a terrace in France. From a football field a world away to here, in France, where he hopes water and rocks will heal. From faraway it all makes sense that long ago a young Bernadette saw an apparition; up close, it seems impossible. But it also seems impossible that one minute he's throwing a ball in a perfect spiral and the next he's on the ground with the connection to his arms and legs forever cut.

Thinks of Jack Traynor coming here after the war during a time when information didn't travel as fast. Wondered how he got here, who helped him, how it felt to be the one to get the prize—to come out walking. Joe says it's state of mind. That Traynor believed so bad his wish came true. Sometimes Joe sounded like a philosopher or something. Mike's banking on mom, leaning on her faith. And the stars ... he looks up. The sky's a cloudy white. Thinks of the stars hiding out there in the vast sky. Wonders at what moment the sun extinguishes their fire. He knows they're there, shining down, even thought he can't see them. He'll bank on starlight.

⌘   ⌘   ⌘

After lunch they take the elevator down to a big lobby with huge, glass doors facing the mountain. Kinda sterile, hospital-like, but built for traffic. The view beyond the glass takes your eyes from the stark decor into greens, pinks, and blues. The beauty of France is out in full force, like coming from black and white into color.

On the path with others, Mike's refreshed. Trees, flowers and shrubs line both sides and cushion the unfamiliar sounds—different bird calls, languages. The people in front of them, a woman and a man pushing an old woman in a wheelchair, speak in clipped tones like Dutch or German. A language with edges to it, not lyrical like French. The air is fresh, a little exotic. Though the path is crowded, there's a hush—a kind of quiet. A still-ness, like the sound between notes. His brothers are acting all solemn too.

"There's the grotto," Joe leans down pointing to the left, whispering.

Mike can't see. The crowd blocks his sight line. They're shuffling, mum-bling, eyes straight ahead, like in church after a wedding, everyone waiting to see the bride.

As they near the curve, the path narrows and the gap between people widens, giving families privacy for their time in front of the rocks. Mike and his brothers approach the grotto like the lion, scarecrow and tin man approached the wizard. Tommy, usually hell bent and fire, is quiet. Keeps his head down. Joe is more scholarly in his nervousness. In whispered tones he keeps a running monologue about the number of tourists, why their hotel is better than the one Mike wanted to stay at on the Avenue De Paradis, a street name he'd liked, that they are lucky to have an elevator right to the grotto. Listening to Joe with half an ear, Mike is like the tin man who can't feel the pounding in his chest.

Anticipating the water that will be placed on his back, water that will spring dead nerve endings to life, he can almost feel adrenaline pumping organs to high alert, readying them to awaken and respond to his signals, his thoughts, wishes, hopes, dreams. As they march forward waiting their turn, Mike keeps his chin up. He opens himself to the energy of the place and prepares for magic if it's to come today. In the line of the faithful, Mike prays.

Talking is more his praying with the drone of Joe's monologue his backdrop. Speaking to God, to Mary, he asks for his limbs, begs for the small, miraculous connection of bone and sinew that will free him from the chair. He tries not to think of his indiscretions over the years, the mistakes, the sins, venial not mortal, that might prevent the gap from filling in. He reasons with God, wagers—"If you do this, I'll go to Mass, make peace with Dad, take care of the family like they do me. I won't be selfish, like when I went to Washington instead of staying at Tremont. I'll be a good father, good husband, great coach." The stream of words and what he can offer is a running tape becoming more strident as they approach the grotto.

In front of the rocks where Mary appeared to Bernadette, Joe pushes Mike's chair front and center. On this hallowed ground, he and Tommy kneel as others did. Mike looks straight ahead, genuflecting in his head, lowering his eyes for just a moment so as not to miss a nuance of breath that might come from the rocks. They stare back at him silently, but he feels a stirring. Like curtains blowing, he feels a wind.

A twinge inside makes him swallow hard. He's tugged toward the rocks, like a string between them is pulling him forward. He feels a connection. But the connection is not in his back; it's in his gut, his soul. The deepest part of him. He wants to lean in, put his face near the rocks, cry. In his wanting, he stares at the rocks and something reaches from inside, from his chest, his heart, and stretches across the small divide, like an arm reaching out and laying a hand flat on the wall. Like he's pulled there, to touch the hard surface worn down by millions of eyes.

Connected, it's as if something flows through him. He can almost feel it rising from his toes to his head. Filling him with what he needs to know. From rocks that are still. Without movement or touch, he receives.

Pounding in his temples, he's dizzy, breathing fast. A fullness in his mind puffs out scrawny legs and arms like balloons filled to bursting that will blow him from the chair. Not by moving, but by lifting, as if all that's inside can carry him to the sky, like the jet engines holding the plane in the air.

What he needs is inside, whether arms move or not. Like silver wings, immobile and strong carrying hundreds of people, he can lift himself and others with his mind, with who he is. His special gifts are meant to shine through his eyes, his face. Though his body is stagnant, his lifeblood is not.

Tears roll down his flushed face, brothers' heads on either side bent in prayer. Looking at the backs of their heads and remembering all the times he's prayed for arms and legs, he knows he's found them, on either side of his chair. He's grateful and wants to place his hands on their heads, a blessing, a thank you, to share the message, the jolt he received.

As tears bundle in his throat, he can't hold in his gasp. Both brothers jump up, all over him, wiping his face, touching his shoulders, asking and asking if he's ok. People start to notice, turn their heads. Not the stage Mike wants.

"Get me outta here," he says, the tears still flowing.

"But the water's up there," Tommy points ahead.

"I can't right now. Tomorrow. C'mon, let's go," Mike says, knowing he's not coming back, that he got what he came for.

Shuffling, they push slowly through the crowd, Joe in front clearing the way. With his head down, Mike sees Joe's sneakers taking small steps through the line-up of those waiting to get to the rocks. Save your strength, Mike thinks. Remembers the tips of the sneakers under his bed when his head pressed into the donut. Thinks of the miles Joe's feet have traveled for him. Of everything he's done for him from that day to this. Knows he'll forever need Joe in front and Tommy in back. Forever stuck to his chair. A sourness rises from his stomach. Without them he's dead. His head feels hot. How can I tell them? How can I tell them?

Back in the room, Mike asks to go to bed.

"Should have napped when we did," Joe says as he and Tommy change his clothes and tuck him in. Mike's eyes are open, but his mind is inside, far away, touching that spot deep down where he knows his path is on wheels.

"You hungry?" Joe ventures a question.

"No. Just want to sleep."

Turning off the bedside light, Joe asks Tommy to go downstairs to get some food for the two of them. He closes the curtains and turns on a small light on the table by the terrace door. Mike closes his eyes. Hears them eating when Tommy gets back, talking softly. He needs time to think. Feels funny inside like all balled up, thoughts coming at him this way and that. Didn't want to be told this is it. Didn't want this lifetime set with his brothers on either side, them carrying him, him carrying them. Needs the hope to keep him going, keep the family going. Not sure what to do next as he lays in bed, in France, with the sweet mountain air turning stale down his throat.

CHAPTER 14

The next morning Mike feels like he trudged up a mountain and down. The guys bring in breakfast, croissants, butter, and wild assed coffee. So strong he doesn't have to drink it, just smells it. Stomach can't take it today anyway. He's sitting in bed with a tray over his lap. Doesn't really eat, just drinks the water.

"I think I'm jet lagged," Mike says.

"You're jet lagged all right," Tommy answers, small bags under his eyes.

The guys are sitting on either side of the bed using the tray as their table too.

"I'm not going back there," Mike says.

"What the fuck!" Tommy says, throwing the nub of his croissant on the plate.

"Cut it out," Joe says to Tommy. "What happened yesterday, Mike?"

"I don't know." His forehead begins to sweat. Needs air. Glances at the terrace door. It's open. "Got this ... felt this ..." he shakes his head. "I wanna go home."

"Home?" Tommy yells.

"Look, we're all tired," Joe pushes his glasses up. "It was a long day yesterday. Maybe we just need to get acclimated, take our time."

"Maybe," Mike looks at the curtains stirring in the breeze. "Maybe I'll sit on the porch a little while, let you guys go look around town."

"What, and leave you here?" Tommy asks.

"Just an hour or so. Need some air." He's weak, empty, like his insides have nothing to hold onto. As if they're draining out, leaving him a shell. Hollow. The tin man without the oil. "I don't feel right," he looks at Tommy whose eyes stop simmering when he says it.

They get him dressed. He asks for a short sleeved shirt 'cause he's hot.

"You sure you're ok here?" Tommy asks after pushing him onto the terrace.

"Not like I can jump," Mike says.

"What if a bird comes along and craps on your head?" They laugh making up for earlier.

"Don't be too long," Mike says.

When the door closes behind them, Mike's alone. On a terrace in a foreign country. Some magic in that, he thinks.

Taking in the view, his eyes rest on the mountaintop, a sloping edge, not jagged. A friendly mountain. He didn't dream last night, just slept flat out like blank, like he covered too much ground during the day and there was nothing left. Trying to remember what happened, he can't get his mind around it, what he felt, thought. He can't remember the wisdom, just knows his path is on wheels for now.

Guys will kill me when I don't go back down there. Came so far. All they did for me. Maybe I should just go. Let them take me. See for themselves that nothing is going to change.

Shoulders start to hurt again. Should have taken a pill. The breeze feels cold but he's hot. My feet won't touch the ground, he thinks, but I still have to carry. Have to bring people here through the chair. Hated knowing it.

Thinking of the stars he saw from the plane, he looks up. He knows they're out there waiting for a dark sky to spill their light. Knows he's going home in the chair. But the charged mountain air invites him to leave some of his pain, as if to say they're strong enough to take it. So he focuses his mind and sends them his stinging shoulders. Pictures needle points of fire hitting the earth. He sends his labored breath, his dead fish feet, the look in his mom's eyes when he can't bear what's there, knowing he caused it. The strong arms of his brothers. He needs to offer all of it and take back with him the connection from rock to bone, the arm stretching from his chest to the rocks then across the sea, the connection of spirit, leaving him with himself, with who he is. He needs the sustaining energy to live in him—his lift—like air under a plane's wings, to help him finish his broken journey.

Hollowness creaks inside him. He wishes for oil. Like the oil fueling the jet's wings sending them soaring. Doesn't matter if I can't move, he thinks. Gotta keep my jets turning, my heart beating. Gotta fly.

Whatever his purpose, he'd live it, his family the blessing, for as long as they can take it, for as long as he can endure.

People are starting down the path again to the rocks. He wonders where the guys are. He's hot. Wants to go inside. Lay down. Looks behind him, sees the curtains moving. No sound comes from the room. I'm alone. Between a mountain and an empty room.

He's dizzy. His head droops forward, eyes heavy. Soon, he's asleep. In his dream, he's on the terrace looking out at the mountain. The sky turns dark. Curtains blow behind him in a whisper. Air going down his throat is cold then hot. A star appears, a single star, and he lifts his eyes to it. A dot in the sky, so small next to the mountain, but he knows up close it can encompass the earth and burn it up with its heat. The star comes closer, a meteor, brighter and brighter 'til it fills the sky and its heat singes his face. Thinks the heat is brewing inside him. Feels it go down his throat, burning from the inside out. A dry heat that he knows is too hot for starlight. That he knows is too hot to heal.

CHAPTER 15

And a new day will dawn for those who stand long
And the forests will echo with laughter.

Led Zeppelin

Sweating through sleep, sheets damp above and below, fever scorches his head. Arms twitch—small bursts in biceps, jerking shoulders and hands. His back is ablaze. Twisting and fighting, he tries to get out of the fire but he's tied like a mummy, stuck straight, burning on a pyre.

Tiny drops moisten his lips—cool, lifesaving drops.

"Drink, Mike," mom's voice wavers, floats above him.

"Get me out," he wants to say. "Joe, Tom!" he wants to scream. Needs help. But all that comes is a groan.

A white heat fills his eyes, but it's the ceiling. Mom's face. A straw. He grabs it. Sucks. "That's it. Take your time."

Wet hair is petted back from his forehead. A cool cloth. The water. Needs the water. Sees it by the rocks. But no, he's home. Smells home. And the pyre goes out and he's left in a puddle. Opening eyes, mom's face smiles down.

"There you are," her face is a salve.

Opens his mouth and she gives him the straw.

"You've been gone a few days," she says pointing to an IV hanging from a pole. "We were worried."

He smiles a weak smile, feeling planted, where he should be.

"Let's get you out of these wet clothes." She goes to the den door. "Tommy? Rita? Mike's awake."

He hears their footfalls. Tommy gets there first.

"Hey, buddy, how you doing?" he leans over the bed. "Christ you're soaked."

"Hey," Mike says.

"Hi Mike," Rita kisses his cheek. "You gave us a scare with your trip after your trip," she laughs. "I'll get the towels," she says to mom.

Mike looks at Tommy remembering being carried on and off the plane, the nausea, the pain, and not much else.

"Did we have a good time?" Mike asks.

"Yea, great. Let's do it again real soon." Tom helps mom with the sheets.

"Can't get a chill, let's work fast," mom says, their motions perfectly timed as if they trained at the same nursing school. With the three helping, he's changed, the bed's changed and the IV's out within five minutes.

When his head is sunk deep in a fresh pillow, he says, "I'm hungry," making mom happy to run to the kitchen to make soup. Rita follows her to help.

"Never takin' you anywhere again," Tommy says laughing, picking up the sheets and piling them in a corner. "Jesus Christ, we came back from walkin' around and you're zonked on the porch. Joe almost had a heart attack. Felt guilty leaving you. You shoulda heard him! Good thing you were knocked out or I woulda done it for you, what you put me through."

Mike knew to keep quiet, let Tommy vent, which he did for a while. Then Mike changed the subject. "What day is it?" Looking out his window, he sees the sun shining. Feels good to see American sun. He's thirsty.

"Got home Wednesday. Today's Friday. We took turns," he points to the cot that's rumpled. "Joe just went home this morning." Tommy comes to the bed. "We were worried," his eyes are pain and relief at the same time.

Mike's head is still tingling as it releases from the fever's grip, like the clicking in a car's engine after a long ride. "How'd you get me home? Don't remember much."

"Don't ask. Let's just say you're lucky we didn't leave you there. Joe was pissed, man. Scared stiff, but pissed. Had to get you home," he glances at the den door behind which mom was making lunch. He wheels the tray over and starts clearing paper from it. "The hotel's doctor gave you something to bring down the fever so you could travel. Also knocked you out." He smiles. "We sat on the bottom deck on the way home."

"Hey, Tom ..." Mike says, grabbing Tom's eyes as he says it, *"You're* the man."

"Damn right I am." Tom crumples a paper he's holding and high jumps it into the trash can. Makes it.

"Hot dog," Mike says.

"Fuckin' Jack Taylor," Tommy says.

"Traynor."

"Whatever. You better get your act together before Joe gets here."

"He still mad?"

Tommy shrugs, "Well after you got sick ... I had to hear all the way back that we shouldn't have left you alone, shouldn't have gone altogether. It's a day flight on the way back, you know. No sleep." Tommy makes a face like it was a hell of a flight. "Fuckin' man—you're the fuckin' man alright dragging us across the world and then freaking out. 'I wanna go home. I wanna go home.'" Tommy uses a high squeaky voice. "'That's all you kept sayin'."

"I called Joe," mom comes in holding a tray with a bowl of chicken noodle soup, and toast and jelly. The smell is almost enough to satisfy him. "He and Michelle are happy to hear you're awake. Joe said he'll stop by a little later."

Michelle is Joe's wife. They have two young boys. Michelle helped talk Joe into taking Mike to Lourdes. She was all for it. She's always supportive and kind. Mike hopes she calmed Joe down a bit now that they're home.

"Gonna beat me up when he gets here," Mike says, testing the waters to see what mom knows.

"Oh, Joe's ok," mom says taking the bait. "He was just worried, that's all."

Raising his eyebrows, Mike and Tommy exchange a look. Maybe I'll tell him I'm grateful, Mike thinks. Nah, he'll kill me for sure if I say that. But with the smell of mom's steaming soup, with his family here in his room, with the rumpled cot, he is grateful. He'd been to France, tried for a miracle, and found one—in his heart, in his home. Forget the tin man, he thinks, I'm Dorothy!

"I'll do it, mom," Tommy takes the tray.

"Need my glasses," Mike says.

Tommy situates the tray then lifts Mike under the arms so he's sitting straighter. A deep pain in his shoulders groans. Came back with me, he thinks.

Mom adjusts the pillow then puts on his glasses.

"Teamwork," Mike says smiling. He learned long ago not to say 'thank you' to his family. At first, it was all he could say with them doing everything. Then mom asked him not to—said it made her feel like she was doing something she didn't want to do. So, he made jokes instead.

"I'm going to call the doctor," mom closes the door softly behind her.

Gulping hungrily, Tommy can't keep up. "Take it easy now," he says.

"Some water," Mike says, drinking long and hard then burping. Tommy doesn't notice, just keeps on feeding. Toast crunches between his teeth, the sweet jelly soothing his throat. Better than a croissant, he thinks.

When he's finished, Tommy wipes Mike's mouth and pushes the tray away. "So, you gonna tell me? What happened over there?"

Glancing at him, Mike doesn't answer.

"If you weren't hanging out of your chair when we got back, you were going back to the grotto whether you wanted to or not. Joe and I decided."

Mike diverts the conversation, "Was Inger on the plane home?"

"Who?"

"The stewardess—the blond."

Tommy comes close, eyes open wide, "I don't remember," he says, shaking his head like there was no time to notice anything.

Mike laughs. They both laugh. Then Mike's face gets serious. Looks hard at Tom. "I knew it wouldn't work, that's all. I had hopes goin' there, ya know? I wanted it to work," he looks to the window, to his trees. "Sometimes I still can't believe this happened. How could this happen?" he looks back at Tommy. "If anyone was going to get a miracle, I thought it'd be me. But staring at those rocks, I knew this was it," looks at his hands limp on the sheet. "Made me sick."

Tommy stays quiet.

"I couldn't stay there." Mike lifts his arms. "This is how things are, how they're gonna stay."

"What do you mean?"

"I mean, this is it," Mike looks around the room. "Me ... in the bed. This is it."

"No way, man," Tommy gets up, "You can't just give up 'cause of one trip to France. Lots of people go there and come back the same. You know the stats. Hell, Joe recited them chapter and verse before we left."

Mike watches Tommy as he starts pacing, a small part of him happy to hear Tommy's not going to let him give up, a small part of him sad.

"There's things. New things every day. There's hope, man," Tommy pulls the stool over, comes close and puts his hand on Mike's arm. Shakes it. "You gotta fight."

Tommy's face, so young, so full of life. Life he's willing to share with Mike.

The light in Tommy's eyes reminds Mike of when he came home all broken and wasted. Tommy was a child and Mike was still the big brother. A fire came in Tommy's eyes at the age of twelve. The spark from it helps keep Mike alive. Like Tommy and his family are the sun and he's a star that needs their light to shine. But, unlike a star, Mike can't hide in the daylight. He has to burn strong to keep his family ignited.

"I found out what I went there for," his eyes tear a little. "There was this ..." he brings his arms up trying to motion with his hands, "... fullness, this feeling that I had everything I need. I didn't like knowing it." He calls for the cup with his chin and takes another long drink. Healing water. Head falling back on the pillow, he looks at the ceiling. Today, its blankness is welcoming. "My life is here. You guys are my life ... for as long as you can stand it."

"Jesus Christ, man ..." the tone of Tommy's voice implies love, dedication.

And Mike knows that for as long as he needs him, Tommy will be there. Broken Mike is who Tommy knows. Who he knows better than walking Mike. In Tommy's eyes, Mike still swaggers.

"Thanks, man," Mike says even though he's not supposed to thank. Wants to reach out and hug him and does so with his eyes.

"I'll tell ya what," Tommy says standing, "next time you get a crazy idea about flying across the world, ask me about the pills first." They laugh and Tommy turns on the TV. "Let's watch a game," he says.

CHAPTER 16

1976

And the vision that was planted in my brain, still remains.
Simon & Garfunkel

Another party in Mike's room. About 25 people crowd in, Mike in his wheelchair, the bed pushed to the side. Open boxes of pizza are strewn on the cot, bedside table, TV. A keg on the porch is drinks.

Girls dance in a line by the window, fooling around singing with Diana Ross to *Stop in the Name of Love*, motioning like the Supremes, all in synch their hands up like stop signs then sweeping down. Motown isn't Mike's favorite, but Joe plays it 'cause the girls like it.

A little drunk, his vision clouds. Or maybe it's smoke from the joint a few guys are passing in a circle. Well, what's left of the joint. There's a small piece of it in a roach clip that the guys purse their lips around, not touching it when they inhale. Mike doesn't know these guys. Came with one of the girls. It's not the first time someone smoked pot in his room. He never smoked, but didn't care what anyone else did.

These guys are ugly, though. Long hair, kinda dirty. Denim jackets with holes all over.

"You ok?" Joe leans down.

Mike's eyes nearly cross as he looks up smiling. "Yea, music's workin'" he nods to the Supremes.

Joe looks over at the girls and smiles. Their hips slide back and forth in time to the music, their bare arms highlighted by a sheen of sweat. Mike kind of dates one of them—Karen. Met her at a fundraiser about three months ago. She's alright—keeps him company.

"Hey, close that door!" Joe yells looking at the den door. Tommy, in his pj's, looks quickly at Mike, smiles and waves, then shuts the door. "Damn kid," Joe says, "Should be in bed."

"He's ok," Mike says, his eyes droopy.

Joe motions with his chin to the deadbeats smoking in the corner. "Who are they?"

Mike shrugs in his mind not saying anything. Doesn't care. He's glad people are having a good time. At 1:00 a.m., the party looks like it just started. People are dancing, walking in and out to the porch for beer, sitting on the lawn. Neighbors are here too, so the noise doesn't matter. Mike enjoys being lost in the crowd, not anyone special, no one caring when Joe lifts the beer to his lips.

"Wanna hit?" one of the long hairs holds the roach to his face. Mike looks up at Joe, whose eyes are level on the guy.

"Who are you, anyway?" Joe asks.

"It's ok, Joe," Mike can see Joe's worked up.

"Jack. Call me Jack," the guy says. "You wanna hit?" he holds the joint up to Joe.

"Gimme some," Mike says, making Joe take his eyes off the guy. Mike motions with his head to bring the joint down.

"Wait a minute, wait a minute," Joe says, "what about ..."

"C'mon," Mike says to Jack, not looking at Joe.

With a half smile, Jack holds the tip in front of Mike's lips, the first time a stranger other than a doctor, nurse or woman gets this close. The acrid smell is sweet, hot, stronger than the smell floating around the room.

Pursing his lips like he watched the guys do, he drags, pulling on air, the tip of the joint glowing red.

"Hold it in," Jack says.

Mike nods, the hot sweet filling his head, loosening something, a door long closed.

"That's enough," Joe says to Mike, then to Jack, "Get outta here."

Jack shrugs and walks away as Mike exhales, smoke coming out smooth, not burning his throat, as if he had smoked before. He's glad he has his mouth and can move it, glad he can swallow, glad he can breathe and inhale, that his nerves reached his lungs and he can get dizzy from just one puff.

Losing his sense of boundaries, blinking, he thinks he can get up, just doesn't want to. Feels like the smoke filled the space and his body's connected. That his limbs are light like he could float. Maybe he always feels this way, he just doesn't feel it.

Motown's off and Morrison's singing a man's song in his poetic voice, *Love Me Two Times*. Mike glances at Karen, but his eyes don't stay on her. Goes inside his head to find Grace, the girl in his dreams.

Joe wheels him near the open door. "Get some air, man."

Mike's head rolls nicely on his neck. Likes the power of the weed to connect him like this —one with himself, with Jack who offered, with Jim's voice filling his head from ear to ear as if he's inside singing. Or maybe it's the bass or the drums but somehow the smoke opened doors to places inside where the music can seep in and become part of him as if he's part of it— one of the notes that has to play for the song to reverberate.

Looking at the crowded room through half open eyes, the sweat, the noise, none of it holds him and he imagines the beach, his beach, where waves are rough on a rock jetty, where a stormy sea rages and wind tousles hair he can reach up to fix. Closes his eyes to see the music. Grace is with him on the rocks. It's nighttime so she comes. Her short, dark hair is flying around her face. He reaches down to smooth it while her gray eyes look up. The color of her eyes matches the color of where the sky and the ocean meet, forming a oneness, a completeness, everything blending, as if they're in a painting. Leans down to kiss her. Lips are soft. Presses on the small of her back. Wants to love her two times. Holding her, his knees aren't weak, they're strong. Strong legs on strong feet, holding him and her up. And the chords are the waves—drums pounding in rhythm to the water crashing, the beat and notes blending in a masculine melody. They're wet and laughing and her eyelashes stick together forming stars. He lifts her over his head, strong arms straight up, small muscles in his hands adjusting the pressure to lift.

Sliding her down slowly, her curves press into his chest. Eyes holding each other, he gets a hard on. The powerful stiffness against her soft body is a memory of such sweet sadness, like the sweet hot from the joint, that the pounding ocean becomes tears.

Next thing he knows, he's in his room near the bed, Joe yelling at people to leave. The music's off. "Party's over," Joe keeps saying, motioning to the door. He takes Jack by the arm. "Out," he says.

"What's the matter?" Mike says but no one hears. Not sure he said it. There's salt on his lips. From the ocean, he thinks. And his eyes are wet. Probably the smoke.

Karen comes over, "What happened?" she asks.

Mike shakes his head thinking of the waves on the rocks. "Put the music on," he says to her. Next time he opens his eyes, she's gone and the room is empty, except for Joe cleaning up. Head spinning like his stomach, he's wasted. Like the smoke lifted him so high there's no place to go but crash. Remembered Grace's face coming down from the gray sky. That's what made him sad—her face, his strong arms. But no, it wasn't that. It was the happiness turning to sadness so close together. Both emotions tied in a knot so tight he couldn't tell where one ended and the other began. Both emotions forming "the wanting"—wanting Grace, wanting his hands, wanting strong legs, wanting the hard on. His wanting is happiness and sadness twisting together so hard he can't see 'cause of the tears.

Looks at his lap. Looks at the stereo. Looks at Joe crashing around the room. The knot unravels and it's the sadness he's left with.

That night, he dreams of her. They're living in an apartment. Fire escape outside the window. On the landing are red geraniums in a pot, like the ones mom plants outside in the spring. Grace sits at a desk facing the window. The back of her neck is exposed while she leans over writing. He's standing behind her and reaches to touch her naked neck. He rubs it absentmindedly. An everyday gesture she hardly notices. It's everything to him.

They live like artists in old Paris—sleeping through their days, going out at night to clubs and restaurants, hanging with the same crowd. A life he could live, not boxed into a 9 - 5. He's playing bit parts on stage trying to build a career. He's telling her about watching the rehearsal of Hamlet today at the theater. How he imagined himself in the lead role. *'But as we often see, against some storm, a silence in the heavens, the rack stand still, the bold winds speechless, and the orb below as hush as death ...'* He tells her he could have played it better. How he wants to be center stage with eyes upon him, using his body as a vehicle to express emotion. Maybe Grace is writing what he says.

Then they're in bed. He's half on top of her, half on his side, her small body against him. She cuddles in like a cat. He holds on, as if she might run. Hard to hold a cat. It squirms and has a mind of its own. Independent. Knows he can't hold her with his arms and has to hold her with his mind. Has to make her want to stay beside him because of what he says, not what he does.

He whispers in her ear. She giggles and purrs. But what he's saying is important so she becomes still to hear.

Then she turns to him and the look in her eyes is inviting, her pupils open and ready to take him in. When they make love, their bodies tangle in joy. Later, when she's sleeping, he thinks of their whispers and knows their sharing is what's most important. That without the feeling of joy between them, their life together would be diminished. But he's glad their bodies fit together too.

⌘ ⌘ ⌘

Blinking eyes open, Mike pulls himself from sleep. It's early morning. He knows 'cause of the stretch of orange behind the trees outside his window. Also knows 'cause the clock on the bedside table says 5:45 a.m. Slept on his side last night. Something he doesn't do often 'cause of his arms—

one goes to sleep under and the other flops on top. But he likes seeing the window first thing, even if the metal bed guard intersects his vision. Pillows behind his back keep him turned. Like a baby, an infant. Another reason why he sleeps on his back. More adult.

At the edge of his mind's a dream. Wants to grab the corner, unfurl it like a sheet, before it disappears like a bird call in the distance. But his head is heavy and the pizza boxes stacked in the corner distract him. Remembers the party last night. From the smoke to the music to the ocean to his dream, he traveled a thousand miles. Body feels it, like after a hard ride, though he never left the room. Like when he used to drive down the shore and he'd fill the tank but when he got there, the needle didn't move. The miles were under his wheels, they just didn't show.

Red geraniums flash in his mind. Remembers the fire escape and the dream flows back. Half awake, half asleep, he closes his eyes. Pictures Grace next to him, her head on the pillow. Loose bangs fall on her forehead above luminous eyes. High cheekbones make her exotic, but there's a simplicity to her beauty. An easiness. She's not hard to look at. Doesn't suck his energy just looking.

Falls back in the dream. Lying with her, their bodies press together in a naturalness that starts at one end of the earth and ends at the other. Blending with her, dissolving into her, he becomes the man he thinks he is. He takes and gives at the same time as they move in the tide of the ocean. Her eyes reach out to hold him. He wants to jump in their deep wells and be lost forever.

His eyes pop open and he's looking through the bed guard, the metal he sees each morning. He looks past it to the window, the orange sky replaced with blue. The dream's so fresh he can smell her. It'll have to be enough, he thinks.

Looks at the clock. 6:26. Another hour before mom gets up. Guess I'll wait, he thinks.

CHAPTER 17

1985

Hang it up and see what tomorrow brings.

Grateful Dead

"Time to get dressed," Tommy says, clapping hands coming in from the den. "Wow, music's loud," he lowers the stereo. Joe left it blasting. Heart stopping disco Joe played to get Mike out of the doldrums and into the mood.

The Beef 'n Beer starts in about an hour in the boys' gym at Tremont. Mike's working to support the Special Kids Fund, a small, grass roots organization operating out of a street front in Philly that helps disabled kids get crutches, wheelchairs, or transportation. Whatever's needed to attend a mainstream school. The latest initiative is selling oversized coloring books for $5 each. With Mike's network, they'd already raised over $8,000.

Stewart, the guy running the drive, had contacted Mike after a reporter published an article in the local paper about the relay races Mike had organized for the Special Olympics. Washington High had a new field, where over 100 kids showed up to race. Mike wasn't feeling great the day of the race, but had to go 'cause he had arranged for Randall Cunningham from the Eagles to come. Kids got to take pictures with the two of them.

When Stewart had called about hosting a fundraiser, Mike's heart wasn't in it, but he agreed to do it to circle his mind back to positive things.

Lately, he thought more and more about ending it, getting off this planet and freeing his family from the drudgery of caring for him, day in, day out. Though they never complained, he could sometimes see the strain on Joe's face (like tonight), or Tommy's sometimes when he had a date but had to help with Mike before he left or when he came home. Wasn't right.

Sometimes, like before bed, or when Joe is about to leave, Mike asks for help to end it. Thinks that if he's tired or impatient, he might just agree. Joe usually has a fit and goes on and on about life and its meaning; if it'sTommy, he shakes his head and listens. They both know one of them would have to help.

He thinks up wild schemes, like putting a rifle to his head and lodging it just so, with his hand positioned on the trigger. Then, like dialing the phone, he could push the trigger down and end his own life. He only talked about this option when the cramps were twisting bad, or on a rainy day with no visitors when his eyes couldn't help but plead.

Sometimes he'd ask the nurses, but they'd just smile, like he's joking. He got pissed off when they'd shrug him off laughing, their smiles all white, their hands moving and busy to clean or massage him, tidying him for another day of life mixed with pain.

At times his asking got silly, like when the "stranger" option came up. Hire someone to do it. Then the scenarios of who and how would always drift to laughter 'cause Mike wanted a female stranger—in a French maid's costume—to feed him sweets and pills one by one. Or a policewoman, who'd strip before giving him the pills. Laughing with Joe and Tommy, Mike's pain would diminish as the camaraderie took over.

So when Stewart asked, he'd said yes, not knowing whether he kept doing good deed work for himself, the kids, or for his family. They reenergized around his projects, everyone pitching in, excited, except Dad of course. Mike's guilt for not giving one hundred percent could hide behind the logistics. Besides, it made the days go by.

"Lookin' good," Tommy says. Washed and shaved, Mike's hair is blown dry in perfect layers on the sides and curling a little in back, compliments of Rita. When they fussed with his hair, he liked it. The dryer's warmth felt good against his scalp and neck. Rhythmic brush strokes soothed him in a natural way—it's an everyday thing people do, getting their hair done. And he didn't have to watch like he watched everything else done to him, feeding, washing, exercising. Hands were everywhere, except on the butt of a rifle or a line-up of pills.

"Turn it off," Mike motions to the stereo. He told Joe he didn't want it on but Joe being Joe said it might help him feel better.

"It's good music, c'mon." Tommy moves his arms in tight circles then lowers the stereo a little more when Mike gives him the eye. Beats and tones fade in the background.

A blue striped shirt is hanging outside the closet with starched black pants folded on a hanger behind it. Tommy unbuttons the shirt and hangs it on a hook behind the headboard.

"What's the matter? You grumpy or something?"

Mike grunts. "Ouch!" he cries when Tommy lifts him forward. Back hurts today.

"Sorry."

"Joe pissed me off," Mike says, his face dark.

"You want a T-shirt on? You feel cold."

"Gonna be hot in there."

Slipping on one arm of the striped shirt then smoothing it down before laying Mike back, Tommy has the other arm in and shirt buttoned in a flash.

"There," he nods as he straightens the collar.

What you do to me is a shame! Du du du dut du du du ... disco spills from the stereo.

"Sick of this, man, can't even dress myself. Never gonna dress myself."

"Ok, here we go," Tommy's sarcasm doesn't reach his soft eyes. "Want me to turn it up?" he asks smiling. "I will if you don't stop."

Mike cuts his eyes to him but stays quiet. Tommy grabs the pants and slips them on, working quickly, efficiently, more hands, pushing, pulling to get the belt on and fastened, shirt down over it.

Socks over the dead fish, then sneakers. Tommy sings and ties the laces in time to the music, pulling tight on the strongest beat.

Shame! Only love can be to blame ...

Mike wonders how Tommy can touch his feet and sing at the same time. Still can't even look at them. They're so far away it's like they're in another land. A marshy land filled with weakness, so different from the land where his head lives, where he's still strong and viable. Except the times when he wants to curve in and die. Hates when they're uncovered 'cause someone might see the deadness.

"Up," Tommy lifts him to the wheelchair as Evelyn Champagne King keeps singing. *If we lose our love it's a shame ... du du du dut du du du ....*

Tommy secures the hand brace so Mike can push the button on the chair.

"It's hot," Tommy says wiping his own brow. "Want a jacket?"

Making a face, Mike shakes his head.

"You look a little pale."

"Just tired."

"I'll put the TV on while ..."

"Let's just go."

"Have to wait for the girls ..."

"Hey, the boxes!" Mike suddenly remembers what the night's about and that he has 400 books to sell. With proceeds from the door, they'd make another $3,000 for Stewart.

"Already in the van." Tommy runs inside yelling for Judy and Rita to hurry up. Rita's married and lives around the block. Came here to get ready away from the kids.

A circus freak. A mannequin. *I wouldn't want to live with the pain ... du du du dut du du du .... Gonna stay forever. Shame!* It's a shame alright.

"Yo, Tom!"

Feet pound down the stairs like his used to—for school, for practice, to play. Voices in the den clamor, gathering purses and keys, mom asking if they have everything, Tommy mumbling. The family—his family—his connection to earth. Can't let them down, he thinks. Barreling in the room—girls all perfumed, jeans tight against their heels, Tommy clicks off the stereo.

"Oh, you look great!" Judy leans down for a kiss. "Are you ready to boogie?" She does a little dance.

"Let's go," Mike says pushing the button, still not in the mood.

"Be careful," mom calls. She always says that. Mike wonders what worse thing could happen. Rolling to the van, not saying anything, he feels the glances exchanged behind him.

"I'm in a bad mood," he yells so everyone hears, then mumbles, "Can't always be the life of the party."

The girls sit up front and Tommy is standing next to him in the driveway as the lift comes down. Mike's cold. Looks over at Tommy who's watching the controls. "Can you grab my jacket?" he asks.

CHAPTER 18

The world was moving she was right there with it and she was.

Talking Heads

Place is packed. People swarm him. First Stewart, all thank you's, and his cronies behind him smiling. Their cause is noticed now that I put my name behind it, Mike thinks eyeing Stewart's long legs and blond hair. He rolls by.

Entering the boys' gym, Mike's nostalgia weighs on him. Though he'd been in the gym several times since the accident, it always twisted his gut 'cause he owned the gym when he was here. Eyes are bright now, with all the attention, the music, dimmed lights and women—plenty of women. And he can look, just like always.

Ricky Don't Lose that Number is playing, but no one is dancing yet. Food is at one end—roast beef sandwiches, potato salad, the works. Mike eyes it but his stomach's full. Ate at home.

Joe and Michelle walk over smiling. "Hey," Joe takes Mike's temperature with his eyes. Tries to see if Mike is mad at him.

"Hi, Mike," Michelle kisses him. "Want to take off your jacket?"

"Yea. In there," he motions to go in Rich Kelly's office, the Athletic Director. Mr. Kelly was AD when Mike played.

"I'll take him," Joe says and pushes him inside. "You ok?" Joe's voice is nonchalant, not looking at Mike, just taking the jacket off.

"Yea, sorry about before—just wasn't feeling good."

"Let's get a beer," Joe says pushing Mike back into the gym.

Friends come over, Father Greene, who he used to coach little league with, Tim Barry, who lives on his street, and some kids he doesn't know—friends of Judy's from work. Cafeteria tables line both sides of the gym where the bleachers usually pull out. Joe puts Mike on an angle near one of the tables so he can see the dance floor and talk to whoever sits down. Across the way, Eileen, who he dated, waves. Her husband is sitting next to her. After Mike broke it off with her, she still came to the house to visit, even after she was married, just to say hi. She winks. Mike nods and smiles.

People flow in—about 100 by now. We'll do good tonight, Mike thinks, beginning to feel a little better like he always did when he's around people.

Tommy checks in a couple times as the night wears on. Mike sits with the Parker's catching up on kids and houses. Mary and Paul have four kids, their oldest now at Tremont. Mike hasn't seen them in a couple years. They ask about the trip to France, but Mike diverts by talking sports, keeping his voice strong, which is hard to do over loud music. Thirsty, he glances at his beer dripping down the sides of the mug. Wants water and looks for Tom or Joe.

"Oh, there's Jenna!" Mary says, pointing to the door.

A woman, about 5'4" wearing jeans that are loose in the leg but tight at the ankle, stands in the doorway. In profile and shadow, she looks familiar.

"You remember Jenna," Mary turns to him, "we cheered together. She was in your class." Mary's face is angles and light—high cheekbones and sparkling, brown eyes.

Jenna Connors. The cheerleader he wanted to ask out. The one he thought about on that day on the field when the blue jersey filled his eyes.

When she turns full face into the room, Mike's back at summer football practice on the field by the girls' school. Cheerleaders practiced nearby, cartwheeling, jumping, dancing with tanned skin and short shorts. Jenna stood out with her great legs and blond hair. She never looked his way.

Hair short now with loose curls, Jenna waves to folks and joins them at a table near the door. Now he can't see her.

The Isley Brothers belt "Shout" as people dance in a circle, arms up, jumping in unison and shaking the floor. Tony Williams, the class clown in '73, is in the middle of the floor going in circles like Curly of the Three Stooges. Tony calls it "The Worm."

Mike remembers when he was the center of attention while dancing and his eyes shine with longing. Watches Tony's legs going crazy on the floor and his heart squeezes. The same floor where he lifted weights, exercised, and played ball. But he smiles, the happiness reaching his eyes 'cause he's still here, with his friends and then some, and they're here 'cause of him.

Looking back to the table where Jenna is sitting, he moves his head to try and see her. Remembers ... her face ... when one time at a dance he was hamming it up and she was just looking. Kind of in the back of the crowd, just standing there while he jitterbugged or something with a circle around him and his date. He remembered noticing her expressionless face. She just stood there looking, not like the other kids laughing and clapping. She had distracted him and when the song ended, he went to look for her, but she was gone.

A small butterfly jumps in his stomach, a feeling between excitement and fear. Wanting to cross the room and say hi, he sees her stand and greet others, smiling, hugging, her blouse revealing slender arms and a great figure.

He starts to sweat. Wonders if his hair's in place. Pushing the button on the chair, he turns and rolls to where Joe and Michelle are watching people dance.

Mike asks for a drink.

"I'll get water." Joe goes to the bar and comes back with an ice cold glass. Holding it to Mike's lips, he asks, "Everything ok? You look a little hot." He takes a napkin and wipes Mike's forehead.

"How's my hair?"

"Great," Michelle says, combing her fingers loosely through it to set the layers straight.

"Thanks."

"Only a couple of boxes left," Joe says. "One guy bought 50 to take to his office. Stewart is holding court now." Joe points with his chin.

Turning the chair, Mike sees Stewart smiling at three women, teeth flashing, about a head taller than the girls. Mike's eyes are pulled to Jenna, who's animatedly talking to Mary. Her hands move as she talks. It's too dark to see if she's wearing a ring.

Tommy comes off the dance floor and squats by the chair. "How ya doin?"

"Great, good ... good crowd, music's good," Mike's eyes are across the room.

Tommy follows his gaze. "Who's that?"

"She was in my class at Tremont—cheerleader."

"Oh yea?"

"Never really met her ... not really," Mike's voice is flat, nonchalant, like Joe's before when he took off his jacket. Tommy stands. Mike sees him glance at Joe.

In his head, all's silent except for a line of thoughts—we never met, she knows me, never visited. Why's she here? Who invited her? Should I go over? She'll come to say hi. And then, as if his thoughts stretched in a straight line right to her, she and Mary turn and walk toward him.

He's gonna throw up.

"Here she comes," Tommy sings and walks away.

Mike's eyebrows raise in surprise but not because he's nervous, or because she's beautiful and the way she moves strikes a chord so deep inside with a memory of who he was, who he used to be, and wondering if she'd accept him now, knowing who he was then in his uniform ... but not for any of these reasons did shock live on his face, but rather because Mary and Jenna take a place on the dance floor and start to dance!

She was heading his way ... had to see him ... it's not just a reunion—it's a party *he* arranged for a cause *he* supports. Was she invited here by someone who told her what the dance is for? Did she read it in the newspaper? She had to talk to someone before she arrived so why didn't she come over?

That look in her eye the night he saw her watching him, did she disapprove? Maybe she didn't like him? Twelve years. No one ever mentioned her. I forgot about her. She knew me when it happened. He tried to remember the faces of all those kids filing past the big window near the nurses' station. Did she come?

Frowning, his line of vision is blocked by Tommy leaning down, hands on either side of the chair. "Want to meet her?"

Tommy's face is so close Mike has to move his eyes side to side to see both of Tommy's eyes. "Yea," he says.

"Well, c'mon!"

Mike's eyes are worried.

"It's your party, man, go say hello."

"I look ok?"

"Go!" Tommy sweeps his arm wide in the direction of the dancers, like Mike used to sweep his arm in front of the mirror when he played Hamlet. Now he's center stage without the sheet draped on his shoulders.

His stomach flip flops. Doesn't want to make a spectacle of himself. With Bowie his background singing *Red Shoes,* and Jenna's graceful movements his foreground, he rolls. Dancers' arms and legs are a symphony of movement. Swaying, Jenna's shoulders move opposite her hips, feet centered in black heels. Her eyes are closed so he pictures himself walking up to her, jaunty steps, not too cocky but confident like he used to be, and tapping her on the shoulder, and her looking up and smiling, then him gently taking her hand and wrapping his arm around the small of her back and guiding her in a sweet dance, their hips touching.

Blood pulses up his neck reddening his face. Keeping pressure on his hand with the bicep he trained through years of effort, his only muscle, he persists in moving forward, though it makes him sick. People turn and watch his pursuit. His "can do" athlete's mind pushes past pain and weakness, and holds him steady in the chair as he wheels up to Jenna, swallows hard and says, "Hi!"

Mary and Jenna stop dancing and turn to him all smiles. Mary leans toward Jenna, "This is Mike," she says or "Do you know Mike?" or something like that. Mike only hears her from far away 'cause of the blood.

Magically, all of what he hoped for without knowing he hoped, and thanking her without knowing that he thanked her, in one moment his hope and thanks come together when she smiles, takes his hand, the one not on the button, and says, "Hi, I'm Jenna. I know who you are." And her eyes look at him like they did in his imagination when she looked up instead of down. They sparkle blue and light and make him feel ok to be on the dance floor.

She lets go of his hand and stands in front of him smiling. Mary dances away, swallowed by the crowd. Say something! A thousand thoughts fly in—used to watch you cheer, I was the quarterback, you look nice, I used to dance, haven't seen you in years, are you married?

"You're a good dancer," he says finally. People move away giving them space and they are kind of in the middle of a circle, but not really. "I remember you from cheerleading."

She laughs, smoothing her hair with a ringless hand. "That was a long time ago."

"You still look the same—great—but, your hair was longer." Too much info, he thinks.

"You remember my hair?" she fluffs.

"Well, yea," his face deepens to maroon. "Couldn't help but notice when I practiced on the field next to you ... in the summer." Pictures blond hair down her back.

"I don't remember much about practice," she says, "only keeping my arms straight and smiling."

Does she remember me in the uniform, he wonders, trying not to look down to his wasted legs to see if they showed.

"You have a great crowd here tonight."

He looks around, "Like a reunion." They laugh. The Romantics bring another wave onto the dance floor with *What I Like About You*. Folks go a little crazy in time to the fast beat.

People near them in a frenzy of movement form a loose circle, as if he and Jenna are in the eye of a storm where it's quiet and still. Looking at her, his hand reaches from his chest, like the one at the grotto, trying to bring her closer. She leans down and they begin a conversation that feels like a continuation of one they started ages ago. Words are spoken he later doesn't remember, coming from he doesn't know where, as if they speak a language all their own.

In their cocoon, they sail through time hitting the high points—her college, where she works, his fundraising, Step by Step, who the money helps, newspaper articles she's read about him, his little league coaching. Their talking is familiar and resonates deep, as if they had known each other forever and were catching up.

Mike's voice starts to fade trying to talk over the music. Somehow she knows and kneels next to his chair to be eye level. He keeps talking as if it's normal, but his heart thumps in time to the Stones' *Start Me Up*. Outside he keeps his face smooth and eyes calm. Inside, his heart drips tears 'cause she's kneeling right here in the middle of the floor. Like she doesn't care what anyone thinks. That she just wants to be face to face with him.

Though he's here planted solidly on the ground, his head is in the canopy of stars he saw from the airplane's window. He feels the weight of them holding him in place like ticklish fingers. Like he has to be in the chair on the dance floor in this exact moment beneath the stars to experience the swirling in his head.

As Jenna smiles and talks, heat sears a path from her eyes to his heart, like from the rocks. Filling him. Mending broken pieces. A connection that can't fix the tear in his spine but sews the tatters around his heart. A sealing warmth that would have tingled his toes, lightened his step, now seeps down as he breathes in every morsel of what she offers—kindness, interest, laughter, sharing, fun, life, life, life. He takes it in with the music pounding, like the blood in his temples. Life connecting his dead limbs, making him feel one with himself, all one body. What's in his head is enough to fill the length of him, like the balloons he felt at the rocks. Overflowing, with enough to share.

At some point, Joe brings a chair. Jenna smiles, thanks him and sits facing Mike, as if nothing is unusual and no one is glancing their way. As if they are alone. She sits next to him in the middle of the floor and continues to talk. Not embarrassed, she looks him straight in the eye, cheeks glowing, legs crossed, leaning over every now and then to hear what he says. She's with him in the spotlight, her reflection bouncing off his chair.

And the thankfulness rises up, pressing from inside out, 'cause what's in his eyes and his words hold her. Not his arms or hands or his dancing or walking, but rather his thoughts and ideas. And their sharing weaves a cloth between them. A knit that's tightening in the heat. Without words, as they talk, he says from his mind to hers, thank you, thank you, thank you ....

CHAPTER 19

April

Oh, we've got to let the music play.

Doobie Brothers

His body jerks with little spasms he can't feel, can only see. On his side, Joe massages his back and shoulders to keep the blood circulating and bed sores away. The nurse massages him in the morning, but every day at five, Joe stops by after work to give mom a break. Spends time with Mike, easing his mind and body.

Through the silver bars that Joe lifts so Mike won't roll off, Mike sees the leaves of the trees out front bending and swaying to a rhythmic wind. It's one of those blustery spring days that cleans the air and blows away dust from a long winter. Makes him want to run, sprint really. Imagines strong feet supporting his lean athlete's body, arms pumping to bolster his speed, hair blowing back. Back in the day, he didn't have glasses blocking the air to his eyes. Back in the day ....

"You nervous?" Joe's voice is tight with the pressure he exerts holding Mike in place while he works. In the background Cat Stevens' voice quivers in his unique way singing *Into White*. Mike enjoys the soft guitar and pictures the precise movements of Cat's fingers rendering notes that are carried to a violin as he sings the word white in two syllables—*why-ite*.

Mike asked for quieter music today, not the rock and roll they usually listen to, like Joe's current selection, The Band, playing his favorites from the time before, when Mike could walk.

When Mike first came home from rehab and began questioning life, death and everything in between, Joe pulled out The Band's albums. With a backdrop of searing words, they would talk in low tones, the voices of Levon Helm and Rick Danko belting *Tears of Rage* from the *Music in Big Pink* album, or *Moondog Matinee*. Joe played a particular song over and over—*A Change is Gonna Come*, written by Sam Cooke. The lyrics say how hard living is but we don't know what's beyond the sky. What really struck Joe was the line, *"And then I go to see my brother, and I ask him to help me please."* They spent many hours listening to that song, figuring out the lyrics, discussing what was meant. That somehow Sam Cooke knew, like all musicians know, what's inside a heart.

"Not like a woman's never been here before," Mike answers as Joe rolls him onto his back. There's no relief in being moved around today—the pricks of heat, the stiff muscles, pretty much stay with him. The pain lives in his mind with no way to shake it loose.

Tonight he has to put it aside. Jenna is coming over. After the dance, they talked on the phone every day. More and more, Mike asks for time alone, including the Sunday after the dance when the Phillies were playing and he asked Tommy and Joe to watch the game somewhere else. That got attention and a few wise remarks. He threw them out of his room, called Jenna and they watched the game together over the phone. While listening to her talk, he watched the pitcher's movements, remembering, bringing back the guy on the mound. Made his usually deep voice deeper.

They talked about everything as if they had to fill each other in quickly. He shared the nuances of his physical condition, what moved, what didn't, which was easy to describe—neck up and biceps worked. Talked about his family and how they took care of him, mentioning only in passing that he and Dad hadn't spoken in 12 years. She pressed him to explain, but Mike couldn't. Just said maybe because he switched schools. How Dad didn't want him playing football; how the more Dad said no, the better Mike played. Guessed they were both to blame for not talking. Now the ocean between them was so big it'd take a steamship to cross it. She got all quiet listening. He could almost hear the wheels turning in her head about how to start the steamship's engines. "You're not going to fix this, Jenna," Mike had said dropping it.

What they talked about a lot is how they would have graduated the same year, she from Tremont, he from Washington, and that he knew who she was in high school 'cause of her legs. He didn't say it like that, made it more of a compliment. Jenna said of course she knew who he was, but Mike said he didn't think she remembered him 'cause they never talked. He said he thought about her and had planned to ask her out. She got all giggly like she was 17 again. When he asked if she came to see him in the train line that rolled past his hospital bed for weeks after the accident, she said no When he asked her why, she said she didn't know.

He called her on Monday around six and they kind of ate dinner together. Well, she ate and he told her what he had eaten. That night, he'd drummed up the courage to ask about a boyfriend, whether she had one. It was the question sticking in his throat since the dance and it came out kind of lame, stumbling over words, 'cause it gave meaning to his intentions. When she said no, he was relieved ... until she said she was engaged but they broke it off. Then, he was back to square one, especially when she didn't say why.

Late Tuesday, around nine o'clock, they talked when she got home from work. She owns a women's clothing store in Center City called the Clothespin. On Tuesdays she stays late to do paperwork. Living on the second floor of a duplex apartment just on the edge of Philly, she takes the train to work. Center City is about 30 minutes from her apartment going south. Somers, where Mike lives, is 30 minutes going north, so through their talking, he traveled.

He likes hearing about what goes on in her neighborhood, a place he used to ride through on his way to games at Cardinal McNally. Gives him a sense of city living, even though she's still in the suburbs. He hears about the line of garage doors in her apartment complex and how her door got stuck closed and her neighbor helped to pry it open. How the woman living underneath knocks on her door every now and then with fresh baked cinnamon buns. How she can walk to the Danish Bakery for their locally famous crumb cake. She said once he tastes it, he'll never eat Entenmann's again. He travels through her words imagining her experiences while looking at the white ceiling, a blank slate where he can draw anything he wants. Including a picture of him sitting next to her in bed, where she sits when they talk, looking out louvered windows to the sky.

On Wednesday, she surprised him with a call. When the phone rang, mom was in the room ironing. Mike answered it on speakerphone and Jenna's hello was like a question, sounding a little unsure. Mom turned off the iron, put in his earpiece and left the room. She never asked about girls, just took it in stride. Unless he wanted to tell her, which he did sometimes, but lately there hadn't been much to tell.

It was sexy, having a woman call him. Not about a fundraiser, not about coloring books and not a nurse—a woman who just wanted to talk, see how his day was. See if she could stop by 'cause she had something for him.

"Sure!" he had said, his heart pumping faster. Women had visited him before in friendship and more, but this was different. He knew it and she knew it, and he cursed his rubbery skin, jerky arms and limp hands that he tried to make normal through exercises and massage. But, no matter, they imploded, curving in, his long fingers longer without the width for support.

She's seen my hands, he thought, but it was dark in the gym. I'll turn down the lights and stay in bed, not in my chair. Should I be in the chair? Mike rarely greeted visitors from the chair. It was too much work and sometimes blue jeans hurt his skin. Usually he sat propped up in bed wearing a shirt, his boxers and legs covered with a blanket. Where he sat sometimes depended on Tommy's schedule. If Tom wasn't around, Mike had to stay in bed 'cause it was easier for mom. Easier if I had my hands, he thought.

He dreamt often about having his hands—dressing himself and being able to get around. Not waiting for this one or that one to take him here or there or move him this way or that. He'd be able to wheel himself in the house and roll past his dad watching TV to eat at the table. Though he'd probably be living in an apartment, or maybe be married 'cause he could work—really work—write, shuffle papers, read, coach, drive—they had those special hand pedals now—hug, touch, unbutton blouses ....

The blouse dilemma confounds him. If he was a regular guy, he'd just take it off. Now he had to talk it off. Didn't take much talking with Eileen, and with Karen he didn't try. But when he was at a dance or bar, his eyes naturally went to the blouses, with women of all sizes underneath. The mysteries hidden there would magically unfold if he could unbutton a blouse. Buttons of all sizes taunted him—white ones flat and small, gold and rounded, oblongs, ovals, black thread holding them tight. Buttons pulling across a full breast. That's mostly when he wished for hands.

A memory he plays over and over is when the magic happened in the spring of junior year—his first time, with his girlfriend, Theresa. It turned out to be his only time. On that day, Theresa wore a crisp, white blouse when she came to see him pitch. Standing on the mound with her watching had filled him with confidence, pride. Walking home with her after the game, her dark hair in a ponytail, he was filled with the smell of accomplishment, triumph. A shiny smell, pure and sleek, that honed his edges and funneled his purpose.

Walking in cadence, arm-in-arm, she looked up smiling, her profile soft with a small nose and rounded chin. His long strides guided them through Grant's parking lot into the narrow strip of woods behind the shopping center, where a creek ran unattended, uninhibited.

By a pine tree in a small clearing where the needles made a soft nest, he had stopped, dropped his glove, and with sincerity beating in his heart to the rhythm of the brook, he had pulled her close, kissed her neck and whispered in her ear the truth of who he was and how he felt. Things he wanted her to know, like how his skin tingled when she was with him. How he liked her laugh, her smell. She had wrapped her arms around him and they kissed. When he laid her down, she welcomed him with the innocence and beauty of a young woman. His arms and legs worked as purposefully as they had on the mound, knowing instinctually what to do, knowing the nuances of touch, like twirling the ball to find the right seam to throw a strike.

With the training of an athlete and the steam of youth, he had convinced them both to pull the curtain back, to be players on the stage of life in a heart-pounding moment of joy.

Back then, his fingers were nimble with small movements—impossible, tiny movements that unbuttoned Theresa's blouse, leading to life itself, to mysteries he had hoped to take a lifetime to explore. Now, when he kissed a woman, and he had kissed a few from this bed, he kissed from a cage, as if lips and face fit through a hole in a thick wall with his body behind it, his mind needling, seeking skin upon skin pleasure, his legs yearning to sidle up like slow dancing. Instead, like cold marble, he's unable to reach from inside out, to join in the pleasure of a moment of shared touch.

Slamming the closet door, Joe breaks his thoughts. "This ok?" He holds up a baby blue shirt freshly ironed by mom. Mom liked him in blue, said it complimented his dark hair.

"Ok, but the vest too."

"The black one?"

"Yea." It's button down, like a western vest, "It's easy to get off."

Joe's eyebrows raise.

"For mom, later, you asshole."

"Henh? Henh?" his brother taunts. "You never know!"

Mike looks away. "Put an extra blanket over my legs—not a white one either," Mike says. Mom prefers white. Says it's fresher, airy. Mike didn't like that you could see the outline of twigs underneath.

Joe's hands do the familiar work of dressing. One arm in, lift, smooth the shirt, lay back, other arm in then button. Same for the vest. When he's fixed, Joe goes in the house and comes back with a plaid, wool blanket and spreads it over his legs. "Might be hot," he says.

"It's alright. Bring that chair over," Mike motions to a leather armchair by the cot. Joe pulls it close, facing Mike.

"Anything else?" Joe asks. "Better music? Mood music maybe?" the eyebrows go up again, a sparkle beneath.

"How about Steely Dan or something like that?" Mike's eyes are checking the bed, the room, stealing glances out the window. It's close to seven.

Squatting, Joe looks through the tapes.

"Just put anything on," Mike's voice is impatient.

"Something ... soft ... not too soft ..."

"Forget it," Mike's beginning to sweat. "She's gonna be here soon."

Joe turns and flashes a brilliant smile, "Barry White!" he holds up a cassette.

"Get the hell outta here," Mike mumbles, lips hardly moving, checking the outline below the blanket.

"Alright, alright," Joe laughs as he chooses a different tape and snaps on Boz Scaggs' *Lido*. He turns it low. "I'm outta here," he salutes. "Have a good time and call if you need me," Opening the den door he yells, "See you tomorrow, mom."

"Bye, Joe," she calls back, applause from the TV. Dad must be upstairs if mom's watching her show.

Lifting his hand in a flat wave as he passes the end of the bed, Joe turns at the door, winks, and is gone.

Alone in the room, Mike doesn't know whether to be relieved or call him back. Maybe I shouldn't be alone. Music is too low. Damn it, forgot about a drink or something. Glancing at the window, he decides it's too late to ask mom to get something.

Dropping his head back, he looks at the ceiling, his eyes going into it. Thoughts are stored there—pain, laughter, love, and he reaches to try to find remnants of his walking self. Who he was before the accident. Tall. He tries to find tall.

But the tall man—boy really—never lived in this room, and now only lives in his mind. The man he is now, straining to live, sometimes wishing to die, is the man Jenna will be with tonight. Raising his arms, small bumps appear beneath the blue shirt. Drops them.

Turning again to the window, he sees the trees dance, their branches alive with leaves. Imagining Jenna's hair tousled by the wind, blond curls this way and that around her face, he wishes he could greet her at the door. Hopes she knows to just come in.

CHAPTER 20

I want to touch the light the heat I see in your eyes.

Peter Gabriel

Legs crossed, her jeans touch the tops of short, beige boots. A cream colored blouse, with a wide matching belt, rustles when she moves. Her hair blends with the cream, making her blue eyes accessories, the only ones other than a thin, gold chain around her neck. Mike can't take his eyes off her mouth.

When she talks, her full lips move slowly, precisely around her words. White, even teeth glisten when she smiles. Every now and then her tongue peeks out with 'the's and they's' and he thinks he might burst.

The conversation stays on track— her work, his work, the room. She says he looks nice. Her eyes tell him she means it.

Working in the city, she takes the train to Suburban Station then walks to 18th & Chestnut, to her store. She opened it about a year ago, and so far so good. He likes when she says *18th*.

Her present, an 8x10 framed photo of six smiling women holding coloring books, is standing on the bedside table. Jenna's in the middle, her head turned in profile laughing, wind blowing her hair back. Beside the photo is an envelope filled with money. Jenna had taken a box of books from Stewart when she left the dance and had sold them all.

As they talk and laugh, now listening to Steely Dan's *Hey Nineteen*, the windows turn dark. Above the trees, the sky is milky—black mixed with a full moon that he can't see but knows is there. Under the blanket, he's hot. Shouldn't have worn the vest, he thinks.

"Everything ok?" she asks, tilting her head.

"Yea ... yea, I'm just wondering if you want something to drink," he says, his lips dry.

"I'm ok," she says, glancing at his Styrofoam cup that Joe left on the tray.

Beads of sweat form under his hairline. "My mom can get you something."

Standing, she picks up the cup. Smiling, she offers it. Taking the straw in his mouth, he sucks, not sure what he enjoys more, the relief of the water or the smell of her skin. It's a rounded smell, sweet, like watermelon. Wants to take a bite and let the juice run down his chin.

Placing the cup back on the tray, she smoothes his hair. Without asking, she pulls a tissue from a box on the table and wipes under his loose bangs.

"Do you want me to ..." she points at the blanket.

"No!" his eyes widen. "It's ok. I'm ok."

Smiling, her eyes linger on his and without asking, she touches his cheek. Coming close she says, "I love talking to you." Her eyes caress his face.

"Me too. I like when you call me."

"You're not who I remember," she says.

"I'm not who I remember," and they laugh. Moving his neck forward, grateful he can do it, he makes a pass. The only pass left to him. He connects. Their lips meet and his mind reels backwards as if spinning fast like a tumble weed. Back to who he was. Back to the man by the pine tree whispering truths.

When their lips part, he goes for her ear, burying his lips there, softly touching with his tongue. She giggles, raising her shoulders. "That tickles."

She touches her lips to his filling his head with rapture, heat, the wind of a thousand dances. A wind that can blow him from here to the sky. With her lips on his, he's free.

Breathing her in, he's released from bondage, the loneliness of his shell. He connects to her soul, sacred, the two sharing energy, life, movement. She fills his empty well until he overflows and is standing on top of a mountain with arms outstretched. On the pinnacle of life he wants to soar into the warm breeze and float on the mysteries there. He wants to fly into the night sky and does so in his mind. All the movement he dreams about swirls in his head and lands on his lips. Hers is a kiss of freedom.

Trying to hold on, his head leans with her as she lets go. Wanting to enfold her, feel the raspy material of her blouse, the promise of softness under it, he can only look up, mouth open slightly. Trying to come down from the mountain, he hopes he doesn't look like a lost puppy, helpless, yearning, his composure lost among the stars.

In his mind, he grabs her hand and blazes a path with his long legs through lush grass, pulling her with him, to him, pressing their bodies together and laying her gently down, his body on top of hers. Unable to lift even a finger, he closes his mouth in a grim line, eyebrows knitting.

"I'm sorry if I ..." she steps back, eyes worried.

Shaking his head to clear his ghosts he says, "No, no, please ... please, sit here," he nods to the bed, his eyes still dark. He focuses, like in the huddle, to calm his nerves.

Tan piping on her jeans emphasizes the fullness of her thigh as she hikes her leg to sit. Blouse rustling, she leans an arm across his body. She's close, eye level, like when she knelt at the dance.

"Take off my glasses," he says.

She does.

Naked eyes draw to each other. His searching, asking, hers receptive, answering. Kissing again, he loves that the tongue that peeked between her teeth is now inside his mouth, delicious, sharing what he can share, mouth to mouth, where he can match her movements.

Moving his head, he buries in her neck, the sweet smell intoxicating, dizzying. Rubbing his face up and down, nuzzling, her purrs encourage him. Finding her ear, he dives into the folds, exploring, tasting, remembering.

Now, his mind begging, he wants to jump outside his skin and take off her noisy blouse. Opening eyes and pulling back, his mind twists with the paradox of being and not being. Hamlet, hell. This beautiful woman came here of her own choice, without his athlete's body luring her. Not being that man, yet being that man is enough to bring her here.

Through his words, thoughts he had shared, questions he had asked, he attracted her. Who he was but not was—the pitcher, quarterback, swaggering athlete—holed up in a limp, flaccid sack wrapped in metal. But who? A mixture, he thinks, formed by pain, endurance, determination. Could he be and not be at the same time?

"Where's Shakespeare when you need him," he mumbles through kisses.

"What?"

"You're beautiful," he says. More kissing. "Those words don't cut it, though. I need a sonnet or something."

Holding his cheeks, she pulls back and just looks in his eyes. Her face is expressionless but he reads volumes. As if she's telling a story through the stillness of her eyes and mouth. She pulls a powerful wind from inside him with the look. A wind that stings his eyes and makes them tear. He feels a beginning and an ending. Like birth. Like a baby pushing from the womb. It hurts, but he's gotta press forward and go into life.

Looking into her eyes, he feels the mossy grass under the pine, smells the pungent earth, the musk in his nose. She brings him the knowing in his heart. Knowing he can die happy right now with her face so close, the lines of her cheeks and nose so perfect, her hair falling forward. So soft, angel's hair. She brings him the man he was under the tree, the man he still is in his head.

He tastes heaven on her lips and likes it. He'd have to tell Joe he doesn't care what's on the other side—gardens, old people. This is heaven. A heaven he'll carry with him forever in this world and into the next. In some ways, he's there already—body dead, head spinning with light.

"You're beautiful," he says again, eyes eating her up.

Tears well in her eyes. "There are some things ... I should probably tell you ... about what happened ... before ..."

"It can wait," he doesn't want to know right now. Doesn't want it tangled in his heaven. "Later. Let's kiss."

They cling together, she with her hands in his hair, he with his mind in hers, until the moon passes over the house leaving the sky in the window an enveloping black.

CHAPTER 21

"You really like her," mom says, a statement not a question.

"Uh huh," he takes another bite of egg salad, which he asked for instead of cereal, signaling mom it's a special day.

Saving eggs for occasions like in real life, when you go out for breakfast on vacation or on Sundays after Church, reminded him of walking, of when he was a kid and dad took the him and Joe to a diner before practice or a baseball game. Or when he came home after morning practice on Saturday and mom had hot breakfast on the table, eggs sunny side up and bacon. Since gooey eggs don't work well now that he wears a bib, mom makes egg salad.

And mom's egg salad is the best. A little mayo, garlic powder and salt, nothing special. Her cooking did the trick—whites always tender, insides the color of daffodils, never green or sticky, and served warm. Before he just chowed down; now he had time to study the in's and out's of eggs.

"What do you do different?" he had asked mom a couple years after the accident.

Shrugging and lifting eyebrows she had answered, "Well, I start with a slow boil, give them time to heat up in the water so they welcome the heat, don't scream from it."

"Scream?"

"And, I know exactly when they're done. I hear ... when their done. I listen."

"To the water?"

"No, the eggs. They tell me."

Looking at her now, twelve years later and settled into his routine, she still hears the eggs like she still hears him, even when he doesn't scream from the heat.

She offers another forkful, her eyes worried, though she says nothing.

"It's alright, mom, she's a good person," he says wanting to add that he knows the deal. That it's a passing phase and eventually the pain will take over. Or, she'll leave. That she's too pretty to stay.

"Was she ever married?" Mom knows Jenna graduated his year so she's 29 too. In Somers, that's old for a woman to be single.

"No," he eats another mouthful then says, "She didn't tell me her story yet."

An eyebrow peaks as she scrapes the dish for a last bite.

After a pause, Mike gives her a long look knowing the question in her mind is the same as in his—Why would *she* want to be with *me*? Usually, he keeps his head on straight when a woman shows interest, knowing it's short term. Like Eileen, who he dated long ago. Even mom knew Eileen wasn't special—he never asked for egg salad. The mornings after, he had cereal.

"I'm worried, Mike," mom says. "I know I don't know Jenna and have no right to say anything ..."

"Mom, relax, she's been here once—it's not like we're getting married."

"That wouldn't be the problem," she probes with her eyes.

"I'm ok," he says. "I'm 29." He lifts both arms in the only gesture he has—his limited range of motion straight up and down.

"You're 29, but not the way she is, or other kids your age—I mean people your age. It's different for you," and her eyes fill up and almost spill over. Instead, she makes busy wiping the tray not looking at him then leaves the room.

His family does that sometimes—thinks of him as still a kid, a teenager. As if he didn't age double time after what he'd been through. Joe says he lacks "life experiences" that change you and make your mindset older through responsibility and living in the outside world. Guess so, he thinks, living in this bubble like a goldfish, looking out and only able to see so much. What he knows and sees is that his little brother is older than him.

Turning to the window, the trees are still. Like him, they wait for someone or the wind to move their limbs. And the wind blew last night in Jenna's arms, springing hope. It's the hope in my eyes mom's worried about.

Glancing at the phone, he decides it's too early to call, that she's probably not even at work yet. Pain nibbles his shoulders then rolls down his back like a hot waterfall. Usually he thinks positive thoughts like the pain's a hot metal that will meld synapses together. Then he imagines the pain making the signals work again. Today he forgets all that and lets it go. Today he looks out the window hoping for a breeze.

CHAPTER 22

"I feel so close to you, like I've known you a long time," Jenna says. Mike's earpiece captures her warm voice, but he'd rather feel her breath in his ear.

"Centuries," he answers.

He'd waited two nights after her visit to call. Didn't want to be too anxious. She seemed happy to hear from him and they launched into a deep conversation, like holding hands and diving in the ocean, smiling at each other underwater sharing moments of discovery, surprise.

She's in her bed looking at the moon through a tall window. From her second floor apartment, there's no interruption to the sky. Said she liked sitting like he sits when they talked, propped on pillows in bed. Said it made her feel like she was next to him. He didn't ask her to describe the ceiling.

He hears classical music mixed with Jenna's soft tones. Mozart, she tells him. Her favorite, that she plays to unwind. Violins are strong in the background, asking and answering at the same time, not playing softly, but rather like fighting. Telling a story fast that if painted would be purples and greens, colors that didn't match. When he said it didn't sound relaxing, she laughed saying the music is in the opening of her favorite movie, Amadeus— the scene where this guy Salieri, who hated Mozart, cuts his own throat. Not his type of bedtime music. He'll stick with Joe's rock and roll.

"I mean it, Mike. We kind of connect, don't we?"

Though he wants to prolong the talk of him and her, he's got the other guy on his mind. Doesn't want to go where Jenna's trying to take him if there's another car on the road. Can't help himself but say, "Hey, Jenna, you're all I think about after the other night. But, I gotta ask...what happened? With the guy you were engaged to? Why aren't you with him ... or another guy?"

After a long pause, "Jenna?"

"You're a guy," she says.

"You know what I mean."

"I don't want to talk about it, Mike. You're ruining the moment. I ... want to keep it separate."

"Keep what separate?"

"I like what we have. Just you and me. That other stuff doesn't matter now."

"Doesn't matter? Jenna, you were marrying this guy. If you're using me to forget, well, forget it," he says. They chuckle.

"I just want to enjoy what I feel when I talk to you. I don't want to bring him into it."

"Who?"

She laughs.

"Hey, we have to be honest. What we talk about is all I have," he says.

When she doesn't say anything, he thinks he pushed too far. Too soon, he thinks. Damnit. Then he asks almost in a whisper, "Did he die?"

She laughs. "No, no, nothing like that. Although my Dad almost killed him. He ... he left me the night before our wedding."

"What?" Mike's voice raises, eyes popping.

"Yes, we ... we were together for two years and ... everything was great. He didn't ... act like anything was wrong. Then, right before the wedding, he started to pick fights. I thought it was just him being him—he's a bit of a hothead ..." she paused. Mozart runs up and down in waves in the background, the music matching the drama unfolding in Mike's head.

"When did it happen?" Mike asks.

"About six months ago." Mike does a quick calculation weighing whether it's enough time in between. "Afterwards, he said he still loved me, just couldn't go through with it. But that was through messages on my machine or through his family. I couldn't speak to him after."

Heart sinking, Mike's throat dries up. Knows his voice might crack. Looks at the cup with the straw's hole facing him, staring a one-eyed taunt. Just out of his reach. "I'm sorry, Jenna, I had no idea. I'm sorry."

"It's ok ... I'm ok. Just a lot to go through. Crazy, mixed-up stuff."

"Where's he now?" Mike again couldn't help asking.

"Around. He calls but I don't answer. His family keeps in touch, trying to get me to go back with him. He's from a big Italian family and they still want us together. They want him to settle down."

"What about your family?"

"It's just me and my Dad. My mom died about ten years ago. Dad lives in Chicago—it was terrible for everyone who had to travel."

"Travel?"

"All the money lost ..."

"Money? Jenna, that's not important. What about you?"

"Me, well ... I lost ... something too. A piece of my heart. I'm still pulling myself out of it. I don't talk about it much because it brings it all back in a big gush."

Wanting to know and not know, he asks, "You ever see him?"

"No. Not at all. I refused to see him that night thinking he was just pulling a stunt, or that it was cold feet, you know. Then he called the caterer and photographer and cancelled everything. The florist dropped off all the flowers at my place ... here. It was like a wake. The flowers ... they were all white ... roses and hydrangeas, my favorites." She pauses then her voice is whispery. "It was a wake no one came to."

Soft sobs blend with Mozart, whose tones are quieter now. He wants to hold her, let her cry while he kisses her head. Wants to stroke her hair and wipe thoughts of the Italian from her mind.

"On what would've been the wedding day, I stayed with my Dad in his hotel," she sniffles. "I couldn't be around those flowers. And, I didn't want him to find me. I unplugged the phone and kept it unplugged for a while. The thing is, now I don't know if he tried to call me. After a week, I thought he'd at least show up at my door or at work, but he didn't. I couldn't believe he didn't try. I kept seeing his car—this silver Camaro—everywhere. But it was never him," she chokes.

Mike presses his lips together, not knowing what to say. The violins played in a way that sounded like tears. Now he wishes they'd fight again and not be sentimental.

"So you didn't talk to him after? How could you … I mean, I understand he's a creep and all but you … you must have been …" Mike frowns thinking of how much he needs to talk to her every day even now after only a couple of weeks. He can't imagine how she cut herself off from a guy she was going to marry.

"Actually, I wanted to die. I'd go to sleep crying and wake up crying. I didn't want to see or talk to anyone. I just went through the motions …" she breaks down.

He understands going through the motions wondering if it's harder if you can move.

"I'm sorry, Mike," her voice is filled with violins.

"No, no, Jesus, Jenna, I'm sorry for … for making you say it. I shouldn't have asked. It's your business, but I'll listen if it helps."

"Hold on," she says. A soft 'whump' sounds in his ear. The cascading music is muffled. Blows her nose in the background.

"Hi," she says picking up the phone.

"So, he's not dead," Mike says and they laugh.

"No, sometimes I wish he was."

"Me too," he said not meaning to say it. Just came out.

"Well," she sniffles. "I haven't cried like that in a while."

"How come I didn't know?" Mike asks meaning how come no one told him.

"Oh, nobody from Tremont knows him. He went to school in Jersey. Mary doesn't know. I haven't seen anyone in so long and when I caught up with them at the dance, there was no reason to say. I had to put him out of my mind, so I don't talk about it. I got rid of the dress, put all of his stuff in a box, and threw it out."

Threw it out? Mike's face is surprised picturing Jenna gathering up, what … shaving cream, razors, toothbrush, clothes, shoes, pictures, albums.

Wonders why she didn't leave it somewhere for him. Or box it up and hide it. Couldn't see her trashing it.

"I had to. I had to cut myself off. My skin hurt when I woke up in the morning." He knows that feeling too and thinks if he could wrap it up in a box and throw it out, well .... "I couldn't even stand to see the clothes *I* wore when I was with him. They made my stomach turn. So, I gave them away and bought new clothes from the store. He never even showed up there."

What's with this guy? Mike doesn't get guys like this having legs.

"For months, I'd cry in the morning getting ready for work. But once the make-up was on, that was my deadline. No more tears. I'd go to work with a smile painted on, like a clown. Like my face was in pieces and I'd have to glue it together to keep it from crumbling. My face didn't belong to me. The only real thing was the lead in my stomach. I was dead inside."

Mike thinks she's him turned inside out—how he's dead outside and she's dead inside. How he tries to change the mask of his body so people can see inside and she's putting on a mask to keep people out. They make a great pair.

"The doctor gave me pills and I'd take one every day. I called it cement because it settled deep inside to keep me grounded ... from not flying away."

"Cement, huh ..."

"It got me through the day when I just wanted to curl in a ball. Then, about two months ago, I forgot to take the pill and I was ok. And one morning I woke up and didn't cry. Then the next day and the next." She pauses. "Sorry. I'm going on and on."

"Hey, it's good to talk about things." Lips dry, he looks at the cup. "Wish I could be there."

"Me too. Hey, Mike, thanks for listening—for caring. It's so easy to talk to you."

"I got good ears."

"I'm a little tired. Do you mind if we hang up? I'm not upset or anything. I'm actually glad you made me talk about it. It's nice to talk without having to watch what I'm saying. Will you call me tomorrow?"

"Sure," he says then adds quickly, "Hey, Jenna, what's his name?"

She doesn't answer.

"Just want to know."

"Nick." Her voice is quiet. Then a little louder, "Nick Stefano."

"Nick," he repeats trying to hear if there was a whisper in her voice.

After they hang up, mom comes in and gives him a drink, lowers the bed and shuts the light. Staring at the ceiling, he thinks about how that asshole hurt Jenna. He tries to picture Nick—Nick Stefano—says it in his mind with a sing song voice, like a child making fun. All he comes up with is a guy with black, slicked hair, a cigarette and a T-shirt. Probably short. From South Philly. Or maybe he's the tailored suit kind of Italian, all tight in the waist with black shined shoes. Probably just a regular guy. But why would he leave Jenna? The ceiling doesn't answer.

CHAPTER 23

May

Jenna calls. She's crying. "Mike?"

"What's the matter?" She's hurt. Where is she? Maybe she's in the hospital or some guy attacked her or she fell ... or ... or ...

"I just ... saw this beautiful store ..."

"What?"

"This store ... this new bookstore ... right across the street from mine," she hiccups.

"A bookstore!" His face is red from adrenaline having nowhere to go.

"I was walking down 18th from the train and the grand opening sign was out—it's been under construction for months now—so I went in," she sobs, "I felt ... when I walked in ... it's this big open space ... two levels ... filled with books. Like a cathedral, the books reached to the sky and classical music was playing ... Vivaldi ..."

"Vivaldi?"

"Not Vivaldi ... Bach ... I don't know ... beautiful harps ..." sniffling, "... like heaven. I was transported. My heart filled up and I thought of you, of when we're together, and I didn't know what to do because it's just a bookstore but all I saw was you." She cries.

"Ah, Jenna," dumbfounded, his heart tries to reach across the phone line. "You sure you thought of me?"

"Hmm?" she hums, like "What?"

"When you saw the books ... sure it's not some professor you used to date?" he jokes knowing she's alright and just having some sort of fit.

She laughs through tears. "No, I thought of you, you jerk. I can't explain. Just that I wanted to buy all the books in the store and read them with you. The store is amazing—it's like all these words and ideas in one place made me think I'd been there before. Where the harp music is real. It touched my heart."

"Gotta see this place," he says thinking she's kooky in a cute way. "Did you buy me anything?"

"Yes," she chuckles, "After the initial shock. I walked around, my eyes wide like a kid in a candy store. Then I went upstairs and just ... looked down, and all the books were so beautiful, just waiting to be touched."

"Touched, huh."

"I found this little red one—leather bound. Hold on a minute," the phone drops on a hard surface. Mumbling. At the register in her store, he thinks. Hopes she has tissues. Her voice fades, "Yes, we have a few in the back. Sure. I'll be with you in a minute." Picking up the phone, "I have to go." Her voice is close in his ear. "I'll call you back later, ok?"

"Don't forget to wipe your face. Make-up is probably all over the place."

"I like you, Mike Murphy," she laughs.

"I like me too. Yea, call me later."

After hanging up, he feels a sense of something—like life. She brought me to a store, he thinks ... a new store ... in Center City. I'm in my bed and I was transported like she was. Maybe that's what Joe means by life experiences. Going through small moments with someone else. Moments that hit someone differently than they hit you. Had to admit that most of his moments were about him. People reflect back what he gives, what he's able to give, or what he needs, rather than asking him to take on their stuff.

I'll take on her stuff, he thinks. Hope she piles it on. His heart beats stronger thinking he'd been part of her day. That she thought of him when she walked in a store. She thought of him. Mom's got a right to worry, he thinks, his eyes wishing they were on something other than the white walls of his room.

⌘ ⌘ ⌘

They laugh. The little red book is on the bedside table. It's a love book, like for Valentine's Day, even though it's May. There's poems and lacey drawings in it. Inside the cover Jenna had written, "I heard harps and thought of you." He's not sure what it means.

"I had to buy it," she's sitting on the bed next to him. Sky isn't quite dark yet so it doesn't feel like seven o'clock. Jenna closed the store a little early to get here. Called him after she got off the train to see if it was ok to come by.

"You'll have to read it to me," he says, looking at the metal buttons on the short leather jacket she's still wearing. "Take off your coat."

"Sorry to drop in like this," she stands and hangs her coat on a hook near the door. "Want some music?"

"Sure," he motions to the stereo knowing she knows where it is. "I'm glad you came over," he watches her as she selects a tape. She turns and smiles at him before clicking it on. *I've heard people say, that too much of anything is not good for you baby ...* Barry White. Shit, Joe. Must have left it on top. He swallows, a little nervous 'cause he didn't know she was coming 'til after Joe left so he's in a flannel shirt. Glances at the red book as she comes back to the bed.

She sits and kisses him. A long kiss making him understand the harps. *It's just not enough.*

"Want to move in?" he asks. "We can do this every night." She kisses him again. "My mom would have to stay ..." more kissing, "and Tommy," he gets her ear, "and Joe of course is here every night," nuzzles her neck, "then there's the nurses, yea the nurses ..." and he laughs and she pulls back grinning.

"Ha ha ... so funny," she kisses one cheek then the other. "This morning was weird," she holds her hand to her stomach. "I was all churned up."

"Imagine how I felt when you called crying," he says. "And I can't even feel." *Some things I can't get used to no matter how I try.*

After more kissing and laughter, "Why'd you put this music on? Gonna take your blouse off?" he looks at her neck and wants to touch where it blends into the skin of her chest. In one motion he could glide his hand from one to the other, then down.

"You're relentless ... in a good way," she says.

"Relentless in a good way," he repeats, "them's kissin' words." He grabs her lips that are just there for the asking.

"I'd like to take you there," she says between kisses.

"Take me ..." he's out of breath. *Just like the more you give the more I want and baby that's no lie ...*

"To the bookstore?" she mumbles.

"No. We got other places to go where you can take me."

"See, relentless."

I feel the change, somethin' moves .... He buries his lips in her neck with a growl, his mind pinning her to the bed and taking her places ... *can't get enough of your love babe.*

CHAPTER 24

June

The TV blinks casting shadows on the ceiling. Mike sits in bed with a white blanket in place, Jenna in her chair to his right. Watching a M*A*S*H rerun, Hawkeye Pierce taunts Hoolihan with his offbeat attempts at seduction. Mike glances sidelong at Jenna. Her half moon smile tells him she likes the banter between Hawkeye and Margaret, their ongoing conversation like foreplay, as if they're naked in bed.

When Mike isn't stealing glances at Jenna, his eyes rest just above the screen, not really watching. Shadows form an umbrella of fantasy over his head. He imagines Jenna in bed next to him watching the show, a bowl of popcorn between them, him feeding her one by one, touching it to her lips, her mouth opening, and him pausing just before placing it on her tongue. Watching her chew, he'd caress her cheek with the back of his hand, waiting for her to turn and kiss him. Then he can't help but fast forward to when they'd get it on.

"Hey," Jenna's looking at him. "Where were you?"

Laughs. "Somewhere fun," his voice is gravelly. "You were there too."

"Hmmmm...." she comes over. "You're always thinking," she caresses his cheek.

"Got to," he lifts his chin to accept her touch. "I live in my head."

With her so close, he's tied up. Brain tells him to hug and he can't. It's not natural he can't touch her. Doesn't make sense. Even after all these years, he can't get it straight in his head that he can't move.

Looking into her eyes, he swallows his desire. Nowhere for it to go. Like there's a leak inside and everything just flows out, like he's on empty.

"Jenna, I don't know what to do. I want so much. I want everything," he tries to keep the puppy dog out of his eyes.

"I know, I know. Always asking for stuff. Can't do anything for yourself," her face is all sparkles. On the screen Radar's trying to right a wrong to Sherman Potter's horse.

"I got all these feelings," he says.

"Don't go all sappy on me now," she makes a face smiling. She glances at the blanket.

"Can we talk about this?" he raises his arms in a helpless motion, encompassing all that is his world, the narrow span of the bed. "Even with all this wasteland," he chinned toward his twigs, "I'm still a guy. I feel things, want things. Still want to be with you, like a guy. A man. With a woman."

Face softening, she leans over and kisses him tenderly, passion just below the surface, her lips touching and pulling at the same time. He wants to jump in. Doesn't care if it's a well he can't get out of.

Without a word, Jenna runs her hand down his chest, him following it with hungry eyes imagining fingers sparking fire, friendly fire, imagining tingles and tickles. Glancing at her cleavage sitting perfectly between the V of her sweater, his eyes lose the puppies and become white heat.

Removing his glasses, she rests one knee on the bed, comes close and takes his head in her hands. With her eyes, she invites him into the V.

The sweet smell of delight and thanks overpower him as he groans, licks, and tastes, diving deeper with his tongue. Looking up, they breathe the same hard air between them. Air filled with tension and purpose. Gazing in her eyes, he sees his man's eyes reflected. Her eyes are light in a cushion. Hot ... and soft.

"I love you," he says not meaning to, just saying it.

She smiles and sits back on her leg curled under her. There's a satisfied look on her face, as if she made a decision. But it's a teasing look too.

Standing, she takes hold of the blanket near his waist and slowly pulls it down. He's sickened and thrilled at the same time. His T-shirt doesn't cover the boxers. She hesitates only a moment before pulling the covers all the way down, his twigs open to the air, a mutilated exhibit.

Holding his breath, he's suspended, balancing on a tightrope. Her eyes run down his legs in an intimate gesture he can feel, as surely as if she touched him. His wasted glory. She touches her fingers to his ankle and then runs her hand up his shin. When she reaches the knee, his eyes are desperate, straining to see what's on her face, straining to determine what she's thinking with her hand on his skin.

He wishes he could feel her touch; wishes he could express what's in his heart. But words have no place in the searing that's inside him.

She looks at him and smiles reaching with her other hand to touch his face. In her eyes he feels more than her hand on his knee. The TV's shadows can't diminish the glow on her face. She lies down next to him, her one leg covering his two. Nestling like he imagined when he fed her popcorn.

Fevered kisses take over and they're lost in each other, swirling, like they have one mind, like they are one person, one body. She gives him all she can give, kissing, breathing, her eyes in his, but it's enough 'cause she gives it even after she saw his legs. Saw the length of him gone dry. She clings to him even though he can only hold her with his thoughts and fill her with shared laughter.

And he's grateful. For this moment, for the passion that still lives in his head, for Jenna laying next to him. Even with her clothes on. He's flat on a bed, tied in a cage, and a woman like Jenna touches his soul. And it's enough.

CHAPTER 25

Dressed and ready, Mike sits in bed waiting for Tommy, who's gassing up the car. Tonight is the first night in forever he'd be alone with a woman in a car. They're going to a drive-in.

When he first called Jenna to ask, she'd answered yes right away in a voice like rippling water, giggling, sweet. She'd been pressuring him to go out more, Mike guessing she was tired of hanging in his bedroom. When he'd asked Joe and Tommy after he'd asked Jenna, there'd been a fight.

"Hey guys," Mike had said to get their attention. Neither responded. Joe was looking at an old album cover, one of Pink Floyd's, while Tommy was setting up chairs for the guys to watch a game. Mike had waited to ask for help when both brothers were there. Had to time the asking. *The lunatic is on the grass* Joe's music was playing in the background, dark and drawn out, with a beat like marching to a grave.

"I'm taking Jenna out ... to the movies." Crazy laughter from the stereo—*Hoo hoo ha ha ha ha ha*. Tommy stopped what he was doing and Joe looked up at him with a blank look on his face.

"What? You mean ..." Tommy frowned.

"I asked Jenna on a date. I want to take her to the drive-in."

Joe stood and came over to the bed. "Ok, ok," he glanced at Tom, "that's an idea. We can do it." Mike could almost see Joe's brain clicking the options. Tommy came to the other side of the bed, facing Joe.

"Not we, Kemo Sabe," Mike said looking from one to the other, "just me and her ... alone." *And if the dam breaks open many years too soon ....*

"No way," Joe said looking hard at him.

"Wait a minute, Joe," Tommy held up his hand, "Let's hear what he has to say."

"He said it! He wants to be alone with her. Just them." Now Joe's looking hard at Tommy. *I'll see you on the dark side of the moon.*

"So?" Tommy said.

Joe points the album cover at Mike, but still looked at Tommy. "He can't go without one of us. How are they going to get there? She going to drive the van? "

"Why not?" Tom said, challenging Joe, his brothers looking across the bed like he's the battlefield.

"No way," Joe said standing firm.

Mike watched, thinking Joe and Tommy are opposite sides of him— Joe protecting the memory of who Mike was, the kid, the athlete, and Tommy fighting for who Mike could be, the cocky, irreverent, popular guy. Together they made him.

"Then, I'll drive and you follow and we'll leave them alone and come back," Tommy said, already thinking it through to show up Joe.

"Why can't we all just go together? To a regular movie and Mike sits in his chair?"

"No, man, how lame is that?"

"It's safer than her driving."

"What, she going to crash or something? I think Jenna knows how to drive."

"Crash? I didn't say crash, but anything can happen."

"Guys! Guys!" Mike yelled, "Cut it out! Talk about the dark side ... this is the dark side of *my* moon, my brothers fighting over whether I can date! I'm goin'! We're goin' to the movies! The drive-in ... in a car ... so let's figure out how."

After the uproar, he and Tommy had worked on logistics, while Joe huffed and puffed saying he wouldn't be party to it. They decided to use mom's station wagon so Mike could be in the passenger seat when Jenna arrived. Mike didn't want Jenna to see the infant being carried to the car by his brother. Besides, it had a bench seat so Jenna could slide over after they got there.

They talked a lot about how to keep Mike upright, with him not able to balance if the car swerved. And 'cause of the bench seat, he couldn't lean back. Tommy rigged a way to strap him in. They'd practiced a couple of times with Mike in the passenger seat while Tommy made wide or sharp turns, both laughing the times Mike fell over, both satisfied when they got it right.

Mom just bit her lip knowing there was no way to talk Mike out of it. Kept mentioning a double date.

It was a risk, him being in a car with a woman half his size and no experience with his dead weight. Mike wasn't worried. He relied on his head, what was between his ears, and knew whatever happened, he'd work it out.

Joe kept running down the list of "what if's" like what if popcorn stuck in his throat, or what if they had a breakdown on the road, or Jenna got sick and couldn't drive or walk to a phone. Pain—what if his pain kicked in? Lots of things to think about and Mike knew Joe would be pacing in his living room 'til he got the call from Tommy that Mike was home. And Tommy, for all his nonchalance and confidence, Mike knew he'd be sitting in front of the TV with mom but his mind would be waiting for the car to pull up. Though he appreciated his brothers' concern—couldn't live without it—Mike would risk popcorn, pain, or an earthquake, to be on a date with Jenna. His first solo date since 1973.

Now, waiting for Tommy, Mike checks the clock and hopes Jenna's car doesn't pull up first. Thinks about how he'll get into the car if she's here. Wants to be sitting like a regular guy when she arrives. Nerves are on end, those he can feel, the cuffs of his white shirt almost covering his hands. Mouth dry, he wants to call mom to give him a drink. Where's Tommy?

A car pulls up. Mike can't see. A car door opens then slams. After a short pause, he hears another car door opening but not closing. Tommy. Leaving the passenger door open so he can carry him out.

"All set?" Tommy bursts in twirling keys.

"What took so long?"

"Checked the oil," Tommy put the keys in his pocket and lifts Mike out of bed. "Guess Joe got to me," his voice strains with the lift.

"Check to see if she's here," Mike says as he's carried across the room, trying not to think that he's being carried across the room.

"All clear," Tommy maneuvers out the door and sits him in the passenger seat. Strapping him in, Mike feels like an astronaut or someone special, with people to do things for him so he could focus on flying the rocket, winning NASCAR, or saving the world. Tommy strapping him in saved his world.

"I got the money and I'll give it to Jenna when she gets here," Tommy says straightening Mike's shirt and fixing his hair.

"That's enough," Mike says moving his head out of the way, afraid Jenna will see. "Close the door."

Tommy does then rests both hands over the open window. Smiling, he leans down. "Ok?"

"Yea," Mike answers his eyes on the rear view mirror on his door.

"Here she comes," Tommy stands. Mike sees her car—a Gremlin—pull up.

Tommy looks in again, "Be safe, man, or my ass is grass." He meets Jenna halfway down the drive. In the rearview mirror, Mike can see the exchange of money and Jenna's pretty blouse peeking out behind Tommy's back. He can't see her face. Hopes Tommy isn't saying too much like giving instructions for a baby.

When she slides into the driver's seat, Mike likes the curve of her legs in the jeans. His heart skips when she leans over first thing and kisses him. Her perfume is clearly a "going out" scent—musky, dark. "Hi," she says, eyes sparkling. Nice to see them in natural light. It's about eight o'clock and the sky is beginning to turn to dusk.

Sitting back in the driver's seat and keying the ignition, a whiff of her perfume lingers. His eyes cut to the window looking for Tommy, but he'd already disappeared into the house. On my own, he thinks, and his insides skitter with excitement and nerves. "Can you roll up my window?" he asks. She does, but leaves her window down for some air.

Pulling out of the driveway, Jenna chatters about work, the weather, how nice Mike looks. The rippling stream of her voice tells him she's happy to be here with him, even though she's driving.

When she pulls onto County Road, a double lane heavily traveled street, his insides churn a little, which surprises him because Jenna's confident at the wheel. He can tell by the way she handles the car. But she keeps turning to him when she talks instead of keeping her eyes on the road.

Riding with Jenna at the helm is both exciting and sickening, like at the top of a roller coaster ready for the thrill, but scared just the same. Mouth set in a line, Mike calls on reserves to get his mind straight. Guess Joe got to him too. Tries to keep his mind on the drive-in and making out. But Joe's paranoia must have crept in to where his dark side lived, where he looked into a well and saw Dad's eyes staring back at his incompetence.

"Hey, Mike?" she cuts through the muck. They're at a red light.

Turning, mouth dry, his nervous eyes relax when he looks at hers. He sees the caring there and even though she's not strong like his brothers, he knows he's safe. He smiles.

The rest of the way he studies her profile—soft—her sandaled foot on the pedal with just enough pressure to make the car go. On her wrist a silver bracelet dangles when she turns the wheel, her short-sleeved shirt exposing her arm. Focusing on Jenna, he forgets his fears, his hesitation, and wishes he could reach over to kiss her, touch the hair on her neck.

Gravel crunches under the tires as they pull into the lot after Jenna paid at the booth. The sound reminds Mike of carnivals and picnics, people gathering for celebrations, fun. Like when his family used to go to Penny Pack Park with the neighbors. They'd all pile in cars, didn't matter which, everyone heading to the same place. When they got there, they'd run to the creek and he and Joe would jump from rock to rock in the shallow stream, mom yelling to be careful. After dogs and burgers, they'd play games until dark and then sit by the fire toasting marshmallows, looking up at the stars. The stars were brighter back then.

"Want any popcorn?" Jenna startles him.

"Huh? Oh, no, no thanks. Just something to drink." When she's a few steps away, he yells, "With a straw!" and she laughs and keeps walking.

They're about four rows back from the large screen where cartoons are playing. In the car next to him, Mike sees a guy and girl watching and eating popcorn, their speaker already set in the driver's side window. The crackling from the speaker outside Jenna's window is Daffy Duck's garbled voice. Daffy's parading on the screen, waddling with his sleek, black feathers. Even he has arms, Mike thinks.

Glancing over, he wonders if the two next to him think about why he's in the car and his girlfriend is driving. He thinks he looks like a regular guy, but soon it'd be clear he isn't when his stiff form stays facing forward 'stead of pushing Jenna down onto the seat.

Looking at the dashboard, he tries to remember the last time he was in a car alone on the passenger side waiting. Forever ago. He thinks back to when mom would pick him up from practice or a game and then run into the supermarket. He'd slump down, knees up on the dash and think about the plays, which ones worked, which didn't. He'd replay his throws, perfect spirals into the hands of receivers. Back then, he didn't think about how his mind and body worked together in a perfect symphony of action and thought. Just took it for granted that his arm would lift and his wrist would jerk with just enough pressure to release the ball, like Jenna's foot on the pedal, to make it go. Now he can't even put knees up, just had to wait.

Door opening, Jenna pops in holding a big soda with two straws sticking out like antennae. The bucket of popcorn is in the crook of her elbow.

She puts both on the floor so she can hook the speaker to her window. After adjusting the volume, Daffy's crackly voice joins them. She slides over and they kiss for a while. This is what I'm talkin' about, he thinks. I'm outside, in a car, necking with my girl.

"This is fun," she says settling back when the cartoon is over. It's dark now, the sky blanketing them. He looks up through his window to see if he can see the stars. Only one or two shine in his line of vision. Knows there are thousands up there and wonders at the enormity of how he arrived in this exact spot beneath them.

"Here," Jenna's holding the soda up for him to drink. He sucks it down wishing he'd asked Tommy for water before he left. After sipping a little herself, Jenna places it back on the floor. He shakes his head no when she holds up the popcorn. Afraid of what Joe said.

Thunderclaps roar through the speaker as the movie begins. *Young Frankenstein* is playing, which is good 'cause they both like Mel Brooks. *High Anxiety* is her favorite, *Blazing Saddles,* his. They laugh at the "knockers" scene, when Igor goes up to the huge doors and is greeted by Frau Brucha's pointy boobs.

As the laughs continue, Jenna eats her popcorn one by one, Mike wishing he could feed her. Whenever she reaches for the soda, she offers it to him first. Lost in the comedy, Mike relaxes, forgetting he can't move. But when Gene Wilder screams from the rooftop for life for his creation, he remembers again, feeling a little like a freak.

Mike's eyes hold fast to the screen when the monster sits up. Swallows some of the crazy doctor's anguish and horrified glory when it rises from the dead. When the impossible happens, Mike's stomach twists. With humor and lightning, the monster lives.

Jenna laughs, distracting him from the screen. Staring at her lips and seeing life there instead of in the grotesque dead man, he says, "Kiss me."

Smiling, she turns and presses her lips to his, all salty and sweet.

"Put the popcorn down," he says.

She does then hikes her leg under her to turn in the seat. Leaning across him with her back to the screen, she places his arm over her hip. He wishes for lightning to bring it back to life.

Removing his glasses, Jenna places them on the dash then kisses one eye then the other then his nose and cheeks. With her fingers lightly tickling his ears and her lips moving softly over his skin, it's as if she knows that touching every inch of his face is touching his body. Knows without him telling her that his face has to do the work of a whole body. That the yearning, the sweet suffering rising from deep inside can only be felt in the tingling in his head.

As the movie plays on, they don't listen. As Frankenstein puts on the ritz, they don't hear. They're lost in each other's faces, tongues, necks, where her musky smell hits a part of his brain that he wants to shake loose.

He doesn't ask her to unbutton her blouse, knowing he already did it with his mind. Knowing she let him in with her eyes. Knowing it doesn't matter. For him, right now, it doesn't matter. What she gives him he takes. And she gives him plenty. Rich, fertile earth that smells like her musk. He sows it in his mind, the garden where everything has to grow.

CHAPTER 26

July

I'm gonna play a little guitar and make it easy to move your feet.

Sly and the Family Stone

Bruce is blasting. Crazy, hot, noisy. At a club, Jenna is on the dance floor with a million others. Mike's craning his neck from a table nearby trying to see her dance. *Spread out now Rosie doctor come cut loose her mama's reins ....* The place is goin' mad. He's a little buzzed and just wants to get closer to the dance floor. Can't see her. Can only see the top of her head every now and then.

The only lover I'm ever gonna need's your soft sweet little girl's tongue .... Where's Tommy to push me closer? Music's pounding in his head. Can't help but close his eyes and nod in time to it. *Ahhhhhhh! Rosalita jump a little lighter. Senorita come sit by my fire. I just want to be your love ain't no lie. Rosalita you're my stone desire.*

Opens his eyes. Sees Jenna with her arms raised over her head, smiling, dancing with her girlfriend. Wants to take her hands and hold them in the air while he pushes against her in the throbbing crowd, then bring them down around her back and press his hips into hers. Imagines the hard on. *I'm comin' to liberate you, confiscate you, I want to be your man. Someday we'll look back on this and it will all seem funny.* Didn't seem funny now with Jenna up there dancing with her girlfriends and him sitting in this chair. Damn chair. Wants a swig of beer. Throat is dry. Looks up at the guy standing next to him who's also watching the dancers. He's holding a bottle of Rolling Rock. Sweat drips from it. Mike imagines the coolness on his fingers. Can feel the wet. But can't imagine standing here with a sweating bottle when he could be dancing, rubbing against a pretty girl. What's wrong with this guy? Mike wants to push him. Say, 'Get out there! Do it for me, man!' If he had this guy's legs, hell, he'd be all over the dance floor.

My tires were slashed and I almost crashed but the Lord had mercy. My machine's a dud, stuck in the mud somewhere in the swamps of Jersey.

"Ah, Jenna, come home tonight," he sings out loud in time to the music, but he can't hear his own voice with the music so loud. Wants her on his lap to kiss her and feel her hot breath and skin. Closes his eyes and pictures her arms around him instead of in the air. *Hold on Daddy's coming.*

Blowing the ceiling off, everyone's yelling *Hey hey hey hey hey hey hey hey hey hey hey hey hey hey Hey!* As the place goes nuts, Mike stares at the beer, but it's a mirage. He'll never reach it. Like he's in the desert walking and walking toward water that keeps moving away. Closing his eyes, he imagines walking in hot sand in a vast, dry place. He comes upon a road that stretches for miles in either direction. Dust kicks up in swirls on the blacktop. Hears a motor coming fast. In the distance, a car speeds toward him. A ramshackle car. It's swerving left and right in time to the chords pounding in his head. Dizzy from the music and thirsty, he wants to run and wave it down, get a drink, get out of this hot sand. But as the chords blend into a single note, the car straightens and speeds past him, blowing dust in his face. And he knows he can't chase it, can't wave or run. All he can do is turn and watch as the song ends and the car disappears into the horizon.

CHAPTER 27

August

"Unbutton your blouse," Mike says breathless, a marching band in his head.

Jenna giggles through lips hot on his, mouths open, exploring.

"C'mon," he whispers.

"No, Mike," she glances at the den door.

"He won't come in ... hasn't in 12 years." Mike rubs noses then grabs her lips again with his.

She pulls away. "Unh unh," she says shaking her head. "It's not appropriate."

"Be inappropriate," he says, face flushed.

"I can't."

"Why not?"

"It's not appropriate to be inappropriate with you ..." she looks around then back at the den door, "... here."

"Here's all I got."

"I'll be inappropriate when it's appropriate," she laughs and though his head is bending inside in a way that hurts, he smiles.

"Let's change the music," she jumps up.

The silky voice of Johnny Matthas is deep into *Chances Are*. His smooth tones fill the room with waves of romance. Jenna bought this tape at that bookstore she was crying about. Has all romantic songs on it. Mike thought he was getting lucky.

"How about the Temptations?" she asks looking through a pile of tapes. Temptations, he thinks.

"How 'bout you come back here and leave the music alone?" Mike asks wanting to keep the mood, thinking maybe Johnny could sway her if he couldn't.

She laughs. "No way. I'm not taking any chances."

Mike laughs, watching her squat to browse through his albums. Thighs fold over calves, all her weight on painted toes peeping from black sandals. White jeans make her figure a smooth picture. The top she's wearing has white ruffles and incredibly small buttons spaced in three's all the way down. Round buttons like pearls, closed with a loop.

"Jenna, c'mon. Come back."

Turning to look at him, she leaves Johnny on but lowers the volume. Back near the bed, she tilts her head and smoothes his hair.

"How're my chances?" he asks.

Pursing her lips she doesn't answer.

"Is it Nick or is it me?"

She turns and flops into a chair that's facing the bed. "What's the difference?"

"Well, if it's him it makes me think one way. If it's me ..."

"How about if it's neither of you? Ever think of that? What if it's me and I just don't want to? That I like kissing and talking and feeling what I feel when I'm around you."

"Look, Jenna. I ..."

"I, I, I. Just because you're paralyzed doesn't make everything about you."

Like when the coach told him he was benched, Mike's speechless. His mouth doesn't open but it's like his chin drops. Not many people say that word around him ... paralyzed.

There's a stretched silence. He breaks it with an edgy voice, "You're more paralyzed than I am."

She looks at him with a long look, like there's a winding road she has to go down in her mind to reach his eyes. "You have no right to say that."

"Jenna, if I was a regular guy we wouldn't be having this conversation. You'd be fighting me off. Or we'd be out somewhere ... having fun. And then we'd do whatever we'd do." Her eyes begin to glisten. "You gotta cut loose from this guy, cut loose from yourself. Use your body ... your great body ... for what you're supposed to—to feel things."

He lets the quiet sit around them, each thinking their own thoughts, not yet ready to meet in the middle.

"I work hard to make my body *not* matter," he says. "You should try making yours matter. You're cut off, Jenna, and I'm the one with a crack in my neck."

She shakes her head and turns away.

"Forget me and all this," he raises his arms, "I'm thinking about you."

"Oh right." She keeps her head turned and begins twirling her hair.

Pausing, he studies her profile but can't see her eyes. He's not buying her deflections. It's either the broken engagement or she's not interested. Either way, they had to talk about it.

"Maybe it's why you're with me. So you don't have to let down your guard. Face things you don't want to. And I can't force you."

"Oh, don't go all Freudian on me," her eyes flash. "I'm with you because I want to be and that's that. If you don't like me being here ... then ... well, then I'll leave," she says it kind of like a question.

"Yea, leave. Go ahead. You can leave, I can't. If I don't like something, I have to stay, work it out. Go ahead," he motions to the door with his chin.

"Well, I ..." she looks at him. "I'm changing this music." She gets up and heads to the stereo then turns abruptly. "Do you really want me to go?"

He holds his mouth in a thin line and doesn't answer. He's steamed being stuck in the bed.

Instead of fooling with the stereo, she comes to the bed. Her eyes are soft. But when she reaches up to touch his hair, he jerks away.

"I guess I'll go then."

"Yea, sure," he says, not knowing how they got here.

"Mike, I ..."

Doesn't let her finish, "You're uptight, Jenna, and probably still in love with Nick." Challenging her, he wants a fight. Thinks of battling it out and then throwing her on the bed and goin' to town.

"Really," she says in a flat voice tilting her head. Turning, she heads for the door, grabbing her purse on the way.

"Flip that stereo off before you go," his eyes are stony.

She stops in her tracks. Turning and looking back at him, she drops the purse and walks to the stereo and turns off Johnny. Silence blankets them. He wonders what they're fighting about.

"I'll talk to you tomorrow?" her voice is a question again. When he doesn't answer, she comes over and asks, "Can I kiss you goodnight?"

Because she asked, his eyes loosen. There's sincerity on her face and he likes that she asked if she could kiss him and didn't just do it. Like she respected that he walked away from her even though he couldn't walk. That she needed his permission to touch.

Unable to stay angry and not really sure what stoked him, he wants her here, clothes on, clothes off. His face is pain, love, agony, passion. "I have no way to show you what I feel," his voice is deep, like a lure sunk in the water.

Her eyes take him in. "You're showing me now. Just look at me ... like that ... and I'll stay forever," she kisses him. He feels her lips somewhere inside him mending a hurt he didn't know he had.

"What's here," she runs her fingers in his hair, "is enough for me."

"For now, maybe," he says. "Maybe in some ways it's too much. Comes with all this," he motions with his head meaning the room, the bed, the trays, the ceiling. "With me you get it all."

"I get more," she says kissing his forehead. "I get what's in there."

Their eyes hold, each looking in to see the other. He sees comfort, company, and laughter, hoping she sees more than metal.

"Let's go dancing again this weekend," she says, her face brightening as if she sees only who he is, not the bed or the chair.

"You're nuts," he moves his face toward hers. "It's what I like about you." They kiss a tender kiss meant for angels. A wispy touch of human skin that bridges lives with threads of silk.

CHAPTER 28

Mom set the table nice and had the food set out when Jenna arrived in his room. Leaning back in his chair the way he had to, Mike's legs just fit under the card table mom covered with a white table cloth.

"It's ok with me if your mom eats with us," Jenna says, after kissing him and sitting down, placing a napkin on her lap and his, no bib tonight.

"She already ate," Mike says not knowing if she did or not. He doesn't want the two women in his life deciding who's going to feed him. Would be awkward for mom not to; awkward for Jenna to pick up his fork if mom's there. Besides, he wanted it like a date—dinner out—and mom made it just so.

Beef stew and cucumber salad. Meat and veggies already in bite sized pieces made it easy. Jenna didn't have to cut his food. She'd fed him before, hamburgers or pizza, but not a meal.

While she talks about her day, she feeds him as if she's been doing it for years. Mike likes that she doesn't make it a big deal, asking him what he wants or getting all embarrassed. Just picks up the food and offers it.

Watching her with soft eyes, he listens to stories of women in the store. Sounds like Mecca, her store. Lots of regulars go there to talk, so Jenna sets out coffee and cookies every day. Mike wonders if guys come in too. Can't imagine they don't. Thoughts like these make his eyes lean back, as if he's watching her from a distance he's afraid to cross.

"....then she bought a house on the beach in Stone Harbor. Lots of money in that family," Jenna feeds him the last bite of meat. "I always wanted a house near the beach." She puts down the fork and looks out the window, a faraway look in her eyes. "I'd like a house where I can hear the silence."

"A beach house isn't good for silence," Mike chuckles. "Waves are crashing all day and night."

She turns back and smiles. "Yea they are," she rests her chin on her hand smiling at him. "But they're quiet. They drown out other things."

He studies her face. "Like leaves," he says nodding to the trees outside the window. His trees.

"Yes, and crickets," she says. "Sounds that leave you alone to hear them."

"Not like cars and trucks on Chestnut Street," Mike says.

"Right," she laughs. "That's why I play my Mozart at night. To drown out the noise in my head." Mike realizes just now that the stereo's off, that he forgot to ask mom to turn it on. "I like loud music too," she says, "especially for dancing."

"Let's put something on now," Mike says, "We can dance."

She laughs. "I should have brought some classical over."

"Whatever. We can dance to that too," he pulls her with his eyes and she stands and leans over. They kiss. Her breath is cucumber sweet.

"You'll like him." Her face is close. "Who?" He kisses her. "Mozart." She rubs noses. "Why?" They kiss again. "He makes you feel things," she says, "with his music." Mike chuckles. "I'd like to feel things," he says.

She smiles, looking him long in the eye. "He helped me, you know," she sits down.

"Who?"

"Mozart."

His eyebrows raise.

"When Nick left, this opera singer I know ..."

"Opera singer?"

"Yea, this guy from downtown. He works near my store but he used to sing for the New York City Opera. Anyway, remember my favorite movie,

Amadeus? He took me to see it the first time in this small, artsy theater on South Street. Did you see it?"

After hesitating a moment, he says, "Nope." He's still back on the point of her dating an opera singer from New York. Who works near her shop.

"I told him I'd go home at night and listen to classical albums while I cooked dinner or just sat and stared. So he said I had to see the movie." She touches the napkin to her mouth and her eyes go faraway again staring into her water glass. "I was glued to the screen. Watching the unfolding of genius, how it supposedly happened. How he'd write his music with people arguing in the background and the sound of their voices fading and you'd just hear the music in his head. As if that's how he heard it, blocking out everything else. I went back four times."

Four times? "Must've made an impression," he says, imagining Jenna in the theater. Was she alone after the first time?

"I just kept going. Then I bought the video. I can bring it over if you want to watch it."

The light on her face makes her look like a child, fresh and bright, and he thinks he wants to hear this music that she loves.

"Yea, bring it over. I want to see the music on your face while we watch." He moves his chin forward and she kisses him. Swears he sees a light inside his head, just behind his eyelids when she touches his lips. Like starlight.

"I just heard silence," she says. Her eyes well up.

Feelings come at him, deep, tangled, gut-wrenching feelings mixing in his head like a brain freeze after too much ice cream. "Are you with me because I can't walk?" he blurts, the words coming from nowhere, everywhere.

The wells dry up fast and she pulls back. "What?" she's shaking her head.

Can't stop himself. Thinks of the opera singer walking in her shop, taking her to the movies, the real movies where you sit next to each other and get real close. "Well, it's pretty quiet in here without footsteps ... walkin' in, walkin' out." He says it in an even tone, not angry, just matter-of-fact.

"What are you saying?"

He's this far in, might as well keep goin'. "I can't run," he says his eyes level.

Gazing at him, her eyes move over his face, just his face, not the chair or anything else. Then they change and he thinks she might cry. Then they change again and he thinks she might yell.

"Is that what you think?" she says finally, her voice not mad, just a question.

"Crossed my mind a few times. We like each other, sure, have fun, but where're we goin'? Trust me, I want to go places but they're mostly places I can't go." He pauses then asks, "Why are you here, Jenna?"

Now a tear drops and he's kicking himself for what he started.

"This again?" she fiddles with her spoon and looks out the window. "I love being with you, Mike. Can't you just let it be?" she turns back to him.

"I just wonder ... I guess .... Is it because there's no threat? Like, we can only get so close. Don't you want to ...? Don't you want to ... I don't mean to be ... don't you want to make love? Be with a man who's a real man ... in every sense?" There. He said it. Finally. Now that it's off his chest it weighs heavier than when it was on. Hurt to push it out there. But if they're goin' one way or the other, he wants to know which way.

"Nick and I had all that," she looks down. "It doesn't matter much to me."

Confusion and surprise mix on his face. A woman so ... sexy ... attractive, he can't imagine she doesn't think about it. Hell, sometimes it's all he thinks about. What he sweats about wanting. What he knows he'll never have except for the eye-to-eye type of skin contact. Starlight has to be enough for him, but can't be for her.

"Jenna, you're too beautiful to say something like that. It's everything between a man and woman," and realizing he just put his foot in his mouth even though he can't move, fixed it by adding, "well, it should be everything ... a lot ... most of what happens ..." he's fumbling the ball. "What I mean is, I've already had you."

Her head turns sharply to him, a frown on her face.

"In my head," he smiles. "I've undressed you down to the very last button. I've seen your body, I've tasted you and buried my nose in your belly button, my tongue between your thighs, which I can still do by the way." The tension relaxes when they both laugh.

"Jenna, you're too young and too ... hummmm ..." he makes a noise like a note, a hum, a plea, no words coming to his mind to describe her smell, her soft skin, her whispers that sing in his heart. "We have sex all day. It'd be nice if once you were in the room."

Cheeks reddening, her face breaks into laughter. "You're crazy," she says and stands and takes his face in her hands. "But don't you see?" she whispers. "That's exactly what I'm feeling ... that we're connected even though we don't ..." she tilts her head, "you know."

"Sit on my lap," he says. She pushes his chair from the table and sits on his legs. He wishes he could feel the pressure of her thighs on his. They wrap themselves in kisses, hot and sweet. Whatever tendrils he has are dancing in her direction with hot sparks lighting the ends. "It's why we're on earth, Jenna," he whispers into her ear.

"Why?" she nuzzles.

"To feel ... to touch ... to share."

In the silence, in the pause between her eyes opening and touching his, in the sound of hearts meeting, he knows her silence, where it lives, her pain beating soundlessly between the notes. He can hear it. In her silent numbness, he can hear it.

CHAPTER 29

October

Lights are turned down in his room. Mom's eating popcorn in the chair where Jenna usually sits. The chair's allowed to stay in the room now that Jenna is here so much. They're watching *The Breakfast Club* on his new VCR. Judy bought the movie, but she's running in and out of the room distracted by cupcakes. She's baking for a sale at the school where she teaches third grade. Keeps getting up and down when the oven timer goes off. After the first bell, she came back with a warm chocolate cupcake for him with vanilla icing melting on top. Brought him milk to wash it down too.

On TV, the kids are sneaking around the hallways following Judd Nelson's character, Bender, the bad guy. Mike likes the guy's spirit. He's bad on the outside, good on the inside. Just hides under tough skin so when his dad burns a cigarette on his arm, he can't feel it.

"Want another one?" Judy comes in carrying a plateful. "These are kind of messed up."

"I'll have one," mom takes a vanilla with vanilla icing.

"The kitchen's a mess, mom, so don't go in till I clean it up," Judy laughs and motions to Mike with the plate.

"No thanks. They're good, though."

Now the kids are in the Library dancing, on rafters, on desks, on the floor. Mike thinks if he wasn't an athlete, he could have been like Bender. After all, it was his rebellious streak that got him to Washington High and on the starting team within three months. Wonders about that sometimes, the strength to change schools in senior year. If he didn't have that strength, would he have the strength to still be in this bed? But, if he didn't have it, if he just followed orders, would he even *be* in the bed?

When Bender and Molly Ringwald's character kiss in the closet, Mike thinks of Jenna. All perfect as a cheerleader, the good girl. Still the good girl. Like Molly to Bender, she's attracted to the good and bad in me, he thinks, and he wishes he could be badder.

He remembers the Friday night before the game. He was hanging out at Bishop Tremont with a bunch of his friends. They were saying things like, "It's cool, man, that you did what you had to do to play," meaning they would still be his friends even though he's at another school. Back then, it was "free" everything. Free love, free to be you and me. Maybe at a different time he wouldn't have been able to switch; maybe at a different time, he wouldn't have wanted to. But back then, it was everything to him.

Mike loses himself in the last scene, when the jock kisses the basket case, when the nerd writes the paper, when Molly gives Bender her earring and closes her hands around his. Bender walks across the football field in his long coat with a red bandana tied around a sloppy boot and raises his hand in a fist. The silhouette distracts Mike because it could be him—tall, dark hair, cocky walk. If I was "bad" and crossed the field in a long coat rather than a football jersey, I'd still be walking, he thinks. Or, I could have been "good" and listened to Dad and not played football at all.

The measure of time is a funny thing, he thinks. The unchanging swiftness of a choice. Is it a long route or a short route to a life decision? Thinks of how fast things changed once he decided to play at Washington, of the separation of his mind from his body and how his thoughts still fly free though his body's grounded. Like dreams.

Thinks of how he's separate from his body, his mom and siblings, but without them he'd be dead. How he's separate from Jenna physically, but how their words, whispers, and kisses tie them in a strong knot even though he can't touch. How the unseen mingling of their hearts sustains him.

Mom finishes her cupcake and licks her forefinger and thumb. Smiles at him. He smiles back thinking of her heart and how big it must be to keep his whole self inside. Wonders how she keeps him and Dad separate in there. He never asks. Doesn't want to know.

CHAPTER 30

December

"Jenna coming over?" Joe asks, massaging Mike's shoulders.

"Not tonight, but I'll talk to her later," Mike answers.

"You guys getting serious?"

"Serious? Ouch." Mike grimaces when Joe hits a cramp that's been bothering him all day. He likes to think the more pain he feels, the better his chances. He thinks it to get through the pain.

Strawberry Fields plays in the background. Joe likes the Beatles, all of their work. Mike doesn't care one way or the other about their music, except for their early songs, *Back in the USSR*, and *Revolution*. Those he likes.

"You can't be serious thinkin' we're serious," Mike says trying to annoy his brother.

"Well it's been like, what, six months?"

"Nine," Mike thinks of how easily they slid to this point. How smooth their flight's been. Liked to think of him and Jenna on a trip going somewhere no one else has ever been.

"She's a nice kid. I like her," Joe says.

"I like her too."

Joe musses his hair.

"Just wondering how you'll handle it going forward," Joe turns Mike on his back. "You cold?" Mike's wearing a long sleeved T-shirt, but the cold outside is the kind that seeps inside even when the heat's on.

"Yea, a little."

Joe rummages in a drawer and brings out a flannel shirt. "Would she move in?"

"Move in?"

Lifting him to put on the shirt, Joe says, "I'm just worried, is all. I can see you're in deep."

Trying not to think of his brother dressing him for bed while they talked about a woman he loved moving in, Mike lets his mind go, knowing he was in for one of Joe's talks.

"I know you love her ... natural for a man to want to be with his woman ..." Joe says, Mike sees her eyes, "... not sure you could be together without us here to help ..." he feels her kiss, "... don't want to see you hurt ..." can smell her neck, "... not sure legally how it would work if you marry ..."

"What do you think happens when we die?" Mike looks at Joe as if he didn't hear any of what Joe said.

Joe raises his hands and frowns like, "What?"

"Do you think I could see you guys, see what's going on?"

"Not this again. What did she say to you? Is she going to help?" Joe's eyes bug out.

"No. No. Nothing like that."

"Why are you asking this now? I'm talking logic and you're ..."

"Calm down," Mike says. "Can you raise the bed and push the phone over?"

Joe does as asked and wraps the strap on Mike's hand then moves stuff out of the way to get the tray near the bed. Another album clicks down. Joe lined them up tonight. Still played albums since Mike had so many. Mike asked for Supertramp, upbeat, fun music for when he talked to Jenna. *The Logical Song* is playing. She should be home from work by now.

"What would happen, Mike? I'm serious," Joe tries to get back on track.

"Now *you're* the one who's serious," Mike smiles.

"Alright, alright. I'm gettin' nowhere tonight," Joe puts on his coat.

"I'm never getting out of this bed, Joe, I know it, you know it, and Jenna knows it. Only way out is ..." he looks up with a playful look on his face. Joe chuckles.

"She wants me to do things, you know, go to her place, stuff like that. She lives on the second floor for Chrissakes. You don't think I think of all this when she's layin' next to me? Wondering how much longer she'll lay next to me when I can't ..." Mike looks down.

"I can't move, Joe, I can't move. But when Jenna's around, I fly. I feel like I'm back on that plane to France with the jet engines under me."

Joe stands there just looking at Mike then comes close. "All I'm saying is, be careful."

Mike sees lines on Joe's face that he never noticed before. Joe's eyes are tired, hair thinning. He's getting older and Mike wonders how much longer he'll come over and play music every night.

A small knot takes hold in his stomach knowing Jenna could never take care of him alone, that he'd always need Joe, Tommy and his family. "Thanks, man. Don't worry about me. Only place I can fall is off the bed." Mike chuckles and Joe smiles creasing the lines around his eyes. "My legs don't work, but my head's in order," Mike adds.

"Tell Jenna I said hi."

Cold air flies in when Joe leaves, the wake of his warmth gone when the door is closed. Even with the phone in front of him, his connection to Jenna's warm voice, Mike frowns and looks at the stark, white walls of the room that seem the echo in the cold.

CHAPTER 31

January, 1986

How does it feel? To be on your own with no direction home?
Bob Dylan

Their routine is that every Wednesday and Friday, Jenna comes over after work. They talk every night, sometimes for hours. Saturdays and Sundays they play by ear, but they usually see each other every weekend. It's dangerous, but he likes it, having someone to call, to talk to, living a little through her experiences. Their connection is strong and she stands up to Joe with her eyes when Joe challenges her with a question that could lead to other places. Places that aren't Joe's business, like about Nick or if she could live in Somers. Joe doesn't do it in a mean or haphazard way; his questions are focused and pointed as he smiles. She pushes back with a soft cushion.

Mike told him to back off, but Joe's concerned. Just like the rest of the family, though they don't say. Hell, he's concerned himself. He's surfing a curl that he knows will crash, but he likes the balance under the slope of the wave. The excitement before he's thrown to the sand under tons of water, lost in the salt.

The wave's not as tight these days, though. Feels the loosening under his feet. It's been since the summer that everyone knows they're a couple. Like he has a real life. Not like Eileen who stayed stuck in the room with him 'cause back then he didn't want people to know he's a gimp with a girl.

Now he doesn't care what people think 'cause he's lost in Jenna's eyes and how she moves on a dance floor when he watches from a corner. He's gone and he knows it. Knows it will be hell coming back. Their music just works. In every way but one. One *he* has to live with, but she doesn't.

She's stuck on this propriety likes she's religious or something. They kiss till the sky's black and she's out of breath, but no more. The buttons stay buttoned and all he can do is pant. There's lots he could do with his tongue except he can't pull rounded plastic through a small hole. Needs her to do that.

For him, it's frustrating like everything else having to do with his body. He's used to it. Used to wanting to do things he can't do. Used to the yearning that pulls him down the well when he wants something bad. Still can't understand how if his mind is so focused and so strong in the wanting that it doesn't happen. His thoughts are weight sometimes and he's amazed they can't press the fissure together.

He's stuck in bed, and beautiful Jenna comes here to be with him. Hell, if she can love him without a body, then he can love her back the same way. She told him that once, when they were in the van on the way to a dance, that she sat behind his chair on the floor as he talked and laughed with the 20 other people stuffed in with Tommy driving. Said she held the metal of the chair as if she was holding him. Said she felt his energy through it. All she could see was the back of his head, his hair black and shiny. She pictured his face smiling and joking, king of the mountain, people all around laughing and looking up to him, enjoying who he still was. Said she hugged him from behind with her mind sending love through the chair. That holding the metal was like holding his hand, and she squeezed it.

Nearly died when she'd said it. They were on the phone at the time. He started crying 'cause he knew what she meant about loving someone through the chair. His heart had to beat through it and now here's a woman telling him hers does too. Next time he saw her, they both cried. Soon as she came in the door, she dropped whatever was in her hands and she ran to him. They buried their faces in each other and wept, hearts hanging out to dry later as they laughed through tears.

Where's it goin'? Joe wants to know, mom wants to know, he wants to know. Wherever it is, they've been there and back and now the road is dividing one way or the other. He feels her slipping away like her foot's letting off the gas pedal to slow her down so she can look ahead to the split. Like she knows she has to choose. Good to be careful before a turn, he thinks.

If he could put his hands over hers on the wheel, he'd turn it so fast toward being together. Knows somehow his wheels could run that road. He'd grab her and let her ride on his lap so he could steer and she wouldn't have to keep up.

But her sideways glances when he's goin' deep into her mind tell him she's not sure. The shortened phone calls, her lighthearted manner when he's pressing into her. Right now he's trying to keep her from a complete stall. But it's hard 'cause he can't reach the pedal.

CHAPTER 32

I can see for miles and miles and miles and miles and miles.

The Who

"Hey."

"Hi!" Jenna closes the door quickly behind her. Rain drips from her umbrella. A cold January rain when it should be snow. She places a small white box on the table and hangs her jacket. Comes over and kisses him with both hands on his cheeks. "How's everything?"

"Good now you're here," he says in a throaty voice. Happy to see her. Was a long day today with the rain. Worried she wouldn't get here. It's Wednesday and sometimes the trains screw her up on her way out of the city. Wish she didn't live so far.

"How's the shop?"

"It was slow today," she motions to the window. "Hey, I have something for you!" Gets the box. Opens it carefully and pulls out a miniature chocolate cake with a cherry on top.

"German chocolate from Rindelaub's!" she says placing it on the tray in front of him. He loves German chocolate cake. "I know you had dinner, so I brought us a treat. Besides, it's my dinner!" She laughs and pulls the stool over.

"There's a knife in there," he points with his head to a drawer near the stereo. Joe left the music on as usual. Upbeat music. The Cars. *It's not the perfume that you wear. It's not the ribbons in your hair. I don't want you comin' here and wastin' all my time.* Jenna goes over and comes back with a knife and some napkins. She cuts a slice then feeds him a small bite. Their eyes hold as he chews.

"Ummmm ..." *I guess you're just what I needed ... I needed someone to please.*

She wears a teasing smile as she runs her finger across the icing and puts it in her mouth, still holding his eyes.

"Come 'ere," he says and she kisses him. "More," he says after several chocolate kisses.

Dabbing her finger, she holds it in front of his mouth. "Open," she says and he's like a bird with his mouth open, waiting. She touches a little to his tongue. He doesn't move. Then she smears the rest on and he sits there, all the sweetness at the edge of him, mouth open as he receives from her. She leans over and mixes her tongue in taking a tiny portion. He's ready to jump through his eyes to grab her. He pushes forward into her mouth and with laughter deep in their throats, mouths pressed together, their tongues are in a swirl of salt and sweet.

So please me.

Later, the cake's away, her boots and socks are off, and she's in the chair facing him, her bare feet crossed at the ankle and resting on the bed. Wishes he could touch them. They're so white and perfect. S-shaped on the bottoms. Pink. Sexy. She rubs them together as they talk.

"So, this weekend I thought we'd go to Joe's. They're having a party, like a neighborhood thing. But no kids. How about it?"

"Saturday or Sunday?" She's filing her nails and doesn't look up.

"Saturday night."

Looking up, "Maybe. My girlfriend, Patty, from Boston may come to town."

"Bring her," Mike says lost in the movement of her feet. He's still in afterglow from the cake.

"Well, I'm not sure what time she's getting here and I may have to pick her up at the airport." Goes back to her nails. "How about Sunday? Can we do something then? Patty's going to see her parents on Sunday."

A fist tightens inside, way deep in his belly where it hurts and comes through his voice in a hard way. "Who's this 'Patty' all of a sudden?"

She laughs. "All of a sudden?"

"Never mentioned her before."

"Well, you don't know everything about me," she sing songs.

He pauses. "No, I guess I don't." Their eyes hold a minute then she goes back to filing.

"Maybe you should leave," he says.

The file stops midair. "What?"

"Leave, go. You don't have to make up stories."

"Leave?"

"It's him, isn't it?"

She frowns. "You think I'm lying?"

He raises his eyebrows making his face appear calm and confident, but inside, his stomach is mush.

Her feet go down to the floor. The file is thrown on the bedside table and the socks go on. Then he knows it's true. "You think I'm lying!" she says head bent over pulling on her boots. He wants to shake her.

"You're not being straight with me," he says.

"You don't know everything about me!" her eyes flash.

"I know what I see and I see you putting on your boots after I make one remark."

"One remark where you accuse me! Because you don't know I have a friend named Patty?"

His mind flashes to their phone calls, even yesterday, when they shared so much it's as if they're in each other's heads. He never saw Patty in there before. Wasn't room for her and him.

You're all I got tonight. You're all I got tonight, I need you ... tonight. Cars keep going. Music's the only sound between them. She's standing, hair mussed from leaning over, eyes sad. Her face is concern—true concern, not like she's faking it, and the sick feeling gets sicker. When he doesn't say anything, she comes over and lifts her hand to comb through his hair like he likes, but his eyes have a shield up so she drops it. Then her face darkens—like the light just drops out of it.

"He's been calling me, Mike, leaving messages. But he's not Patty. She's my friend, who's real, who I guess I just never mentioned."

The chocolate turns sour inside. So fast going from light sweetness to lead. He could cry, but he won't let her see. He feels like he's in Church, when he was a kid and looked up at the statues. Their stares were blank, but he could see pain behind their faces. Sometimes it made him want to cry, but he never did.

"I haven't talked to him," she says, "but ... sometimes ... when I hear his voice I want to pick up the phone ..."

And a light goes out somewhere inside him. The burning, the torch that warmed him is snuffed when he hears her say it. But she keeps talking not seeing what it's doing to him.

"...talk things over, but you stop me. My arm won't move to pick up. I asked Patty to come. To help me sort things out. I don't know if I can ..." she shrugs, looks at the bed then she comes close, her eyes moving from one to the other of his like she's searching in his head for an answer. It's the only place on his body she can search for what he feels. But his eyes are hard and he doesn't let her dig.

You're all I got tonight so be true, tonight. "Why didn't you tell me?" he asks.

"There was nothing to tell ... I didn't want to ruin ..." she waves her hand from him to her, "I didn't want to upset you for nothing."

"For nothing? Nothing? So, you're waiting for it to be something before you tell me?" He looks at his feet, mild lumps under the covers that he no longer hides under a plaid blanket. Just the white like mom likes. "I knew anyway. I could tell somethin' was up."

"Mike, I just need a little time."

"Well, I got plenty of that. Just take what you need and go." Rain beats on the roof in time to the music. *I ... I need you ... tonight.* "Just go," he looks into eyes he could drown in, or maybe it's the rain.

"I can't leave you like this," her eyes caress him but he doesn't want to feel it. Now he's pushing back not to feel.

"We'll talk later. After your weekend with your friend. See what you two come up with," he says in a low voice, thinking it should be him helping her figure it out and how it could never be him.

"I'll call you tomorrow," she says a small smile on her mouth. Glances at the box with the cake in it. "Should I ..."

"Mom'll take care of it," he says.

Putting on her coat, she turns and looks at him while she buttons it, but doesn't come back to kiss him goodbye.

"Goodnight," she says and leaves. He hears her car door then sees the lights u-turn and disappear.

Empty. The room is empty, his heart is empty, his head is empty. Can't think any thoughts. Doesn't want to cry. Anger won't let him anyway. Mom'll know something's wrong 'cause Jenna left so early. Won't ask and I won't tell. Gotta focus on something else. Gotta get through this.

Eyes go up to the ceiling. His friend, confidante. All his thoughts stored there. All the pain, drama, laughter, love played out in the room comes down to this. Jenna's halfway gone and he knows it. He knows there'll be the gradual shift—lessened phone calls, visits. Talk will be more general, hi, how ya doin' kind of thing. Like the tide going down, he won't see it happen all at once, but he'll know when it's out.

CHAPTER 33

They're at a party at a friend of Joe's. Michelle and Jenna are over by the window talking while Mike sits with a group of guys who are discussing politics. Reganomics. He doesn't give a shit about it. What he cares about is the sliding under him—a wet road turning to mud, pulling him down into muck he can't see his way out of.

Last weekend, Jenna didn't come over at all. Even though he told her not to, he didn't expect her to stick to it. Her believed her friend Patty somebody or other came in 'cause she gave specifics. But he didn't like the impatience in her voice when he asked why they couldn't stop by. Then, when he suggested that Tommy drive him somewhere to meet in the middle, she hit the ceiling. Said that the one time she doesn't come over, he makes an effort to come her way. Never asked him before to drive halfway; always said she didn't mind coming over. None of it made sense, except for the reason Mike didn't want to think about.

On Wednesday, a storm blew in so when she arrived at the party tonight, it was their first time together since the cake. They met at the party because Jenna worked late and it was easier than coming all the way to his house. She seemed the same. He was a little standoffish, but she didn't act like she noticed. Using body language is hard when you can't move.

The people around him look old—they're in their 40's. They have houses, kids, mortgages. No wonder they're talking about Regan. But Mike's closed off from that world and is only focused on what's happening between him and Jenna. Even sports talk couldn't get his attention lately.

Jenna works her way over to him. Seems happy and all. Music is on but it's nothing he recognizes. No one dances. Everyone just drinks and talks.

She's sitting on the arm of a chair leaning his way, asking if he wants anything. Her white sweater looks soft and he imagines touching it, feeling the fabric under his fingers, her skin warming it. She offers her beer and he sips. She looks at him long and hard, her face expressionless except for what she's saying with her eyes. And what she's saying is she's with him and wants to be with him. The look is the old Jenna. His stomach twirls and he wants to smile but he can't 'cause he's on the edge of a bottomless pit.

When it's time to leave, they say their goodbyes and Joe pushes him to the van telling Jenna to follow them. She says she has to stop at 7/11 and she'd be over after. The van's quiet on the way home, except for Michelle doing a recap of who lives where, who didn't show, things like that.

Joe gets him in bed while mom and Michelle talk in the other room.

"You upset about something?" Joe asks.

"I'm ok."

"Everything alright with Jenna?"

"Don't know. I'll talk to her about it tonight." Mike keeps his eyes on the bed. Doesn't want to meet Joe's eyes.

"Ok. I'll be over for the game tomorrow," Joe pats his shoulder. Michelle comes in closing the den door behind her, gives him a kiss on the cheek, and they leave.

A tomb, I'm in a tomb. Mike wants to pace the floor. Bites his lip instead. Don't pick a fight, man, just try to talk. Maybe I'm jumping way ahead here. She's been through a lot. But he knows what he knows. Nick's around. He can smell him. Looks out the window. Street is dark.

I knew this goin' in, he thinks. She didn't lie to me about him. But she loves me, I know it. How could she love me? Glances at his feet. Who am I kiddin' ... this was a jump off a cliff. Exciting at the top, hell on the bottom.

Checking the clock, it's 20 minutes since Joe left. Where is she? Did she get lost? Maybe something happened. His mind races thinking where she could be. At 30 minutes, he wants to call mom, Joe, do something.

Then he sees car lights. Door slams. Sees her in the glass through the door holding a Slurpee and a bag.

"Hey," she comes in all nonchalant but he knows something's up. "Got you cherry," she holds up the drink. In her other hand is a flat, brown bag.

"Where were you?"

"At 7/11 ... I told you ..."

"Took a while," his eyebrows raise and his head tilts back.

"I ... had a few things to pick up."

"At midnight? C'mon, Jenna." he tries to take the edge from his voice but it's there, razor sharp.

She puts the bag and the Slurpee on the tray and pushes it over the bed. He ignores her when she offers the drink. Too cold for ice. She sits on the stool, leather jacket still on. "I had to make a phone call."

Now he knows. It's what he thinks but he doesn't want to say. His eyes are hard but he loses the edge in his voice 'cause his throat turns to mush. He can't speak.

"Mike ..." her face tightens. Then, she fills up.

"Ah, shit," he closes his eyes and shakes his head as if to make it all go away. "Don't do this to me," but he can't go into that mushy place. There's a swamp inside him ready to suck him down.

"I don't know what to do," she bursts into tears. "He came over on Monday night."

And the swamp disappears and anger turns his insides to stone. His eyes flash, "You saw him? Been seeing him? All week?" His neck craned so far he thought he might roll himself off the bed.

"No, Mike, no, just Monday, and ... and last night we met up just to talk," she takes a tissue and wipes her eyes.

"Well, that's it then," he's looking down but he doesn't see anything but what an ass he's been for thinking this could work. For wanting a real life. For risking, getting lost in her. For loving. Should have known with her so bottlenecked in her clothes. But he knew her, or thought he did, and knew that he broke through with his eyes. That he touched deep inside to a place

Nick can't reach, even though he can move. "He'll hurt you, Jenna. Never mind me stuck in the bed, he's bad news. He'll hurt you again."

Sobbing, she takes another tissue. He's hot and dry inside his head. Dry as a desert with sand blowing 'round stinging.

"I don't know if we're getting back together," she sniffles.

"Doesn't matter. You lied to me by not telling."

"I didn't know what to do. I want to be with you. But, he ... he ..."

"Yea, he ... he ..." Pictured Nick coming to her apartment, her opening the door. Did she hug him? Fall in his arms? Or did she just open it and walk up the stairs with him behind her watching her ass on the way up? Just picturing him walking up the stairs pulled the start of a chain saw inside. Trying not to see what may have happened when he's up there, the chain saw's swinging like in Texas.

Must have shown on his face 'cause she stands and says, "I have to go," she's still crying. "I'm sorry, Mike." Heads for the door. Without turning she says, "I'll call you tomorrow." The door slams.

He's worked up. No place to go. Looks at the den door and hopes mom doesn't come in. Doesn't want her to see.

Mouth is dry. Stares at the bag Jenna left on the tray. Can't tell what's in it. Wonders if he should have let her talk, kept his cool. But she came here with Nick all over her. Brought him in here, into *his* room.

Wants to sweep everything off the tray, the Slurpee, the bag. Wants to stomp around. Wants to break a window, let in the air. All he can do is sit, breathe hard, and sit. Wishes Tommy was home to talk it through. Glances at the phone. Can't even call. If mom asks, I'll say we had a fight. Doesn't usually ask. Tommy would. I need some air.

He drops his head back on the pillow. The ceiling stares back, like always. White, blank. Closing up, he sucks in the feelings he has for Jenna, like folding in the ripped edges of his heart. Wants to be blank, like the ceiling ... and white. Like the color that's all colors, he'll absorb his thoughts and heartache and tuck them into a neat package that doesn't show. He'll be blank. And white. And he won't tell anything. For now, like the bag on the tray, he'll need someone else to open him up to see what's inside.

CHAPTER 34

March

Like taffy, their parting is gooey, sticky. Holes in certain places, droopy connections in others. Salt water taffy is more like it with the tears mixed in. Hers mostly. Mike dried up like cardboard, boxing it around him so he could hunker down and take the blows. Problem is, her tears drip through and when they touch his skin, they sizzle.

Phone calls aren't every day now. Haven't been in a while but Mike brushes it off and pretends it's something Jenna has to go through to shut Nick out if she's ever going to be able to start something new. Knows they go out. She tells him, but not too much. Just that they go, so she's not lying to him. She still comes over on Wednesday's but weekends are a question. One he doesn't ask. Just waits for her to say, like a doormat waiting for someone to wipe their shoes. But she doesn't wipe. Never treats him like that 'cause she's honest. He just pictures himself on the floor with her shoes on him, willing to have them there, willing to wait.

Tonight she's coming over. And it's not even Wednesday. He's dressed, Bruce is on, Mike asking for music that's masculine. Needs Bruce's strong voice and raunchy notes. *Tenth Avenue Freeze-Out* is playing. Yea, I'm gettin' the freeze out, he thinks. He remembers when the waters were warm and the breezes in his head blew tropical, palm trees swaying. Now, it's the touch and glide, like on ice. Kisses don't give back and forth like they used to. Now, they both hold their oceans in tow so the waves don't crash and mix them up in the sand. *Seemed like the whole world walkin' pretty and you can't find the room to move.* Car's out front. Sees the slope of the hatch and has a feeling it might be the last time the Gremlin's here.

"Hi," she says, bringing in a block of cold air that's not her, but winter trying to hang on and not give into spring. Takes off her gloves and coat. Face is red. Blustery red, not crying red. The way she's smiling reminds him of the nurses back when they were with him. When they came in and pity was just behind their eyes.

"Brrrrrrr, it's cold out there," she says rubbing her hands together. "I don't want to touch you with these ice cubes," holds them up.

Mike nods. *And I got my back to the wall.* "How was your day?" he says all formal, polite. Mom made hot chocolate and Jenna's cup has a lid to keep it warm.

"May I?" she asks like they're just meeting and they never had tongues down each other's throats. He just watches. *Tenth Avenue freeze-out.*

She takes the cup and sits down in the leather chair facing him. Sips a couple of times. "Want any?" she points to his cup.

"Jenna ..." he pauses knowing this is the end, that he's gonna cut her loose, free her from his chair. "I've been thinking ...."

She sips, eyes over the cup watchful like she's waiting for a throw she can catch.

He knows the drill. "This isn't working. Our phone calls ..." he looks at the phone on the tray, "well ... I just don't think we should talk as much anymore. And maybe you don't come over for a while." Throws a perfect spiral. As dangerous as the one he threw on the field that landed him on the bed.

She catches. "I know what you mean," she puts the cup on the bedside table. "Sometimes I feel like ... like we said so much ... there's nothing left to say."

"I can't be your girlfriend," he shakes his head, "I don't wanna know about him and you."

She looks down. He hears the tears. Don't, don't, he thinks. Don't wet my box. He tries to crawl in, but the space is too small, he can't fold his limbs to get inside. Any way he tries, he can't fit. *I walked into a Tenth Avenue freeze-out.*

Jenna comes over and hugs him and they're both crying now, like they're the last people on earth and they know they're gonna die and nothing they can do or say will stop the destruction.

Wet faces, they kiss. She hugs him so tight the ocean bursts inside him and salt is everywhere. He can't see 'cause of it. He pulls his head back to stop from drowning.

"You gotta go, Jenna, you gotta go."

Sobbing, she grabs a tissue and instead of blowing her nose, blows his.

"I wish ..." she doesn't leave his eyes. Doesn't look down to the twigs.

"Yea, me too. All the time." And his eyes reach out, though he tries to hold them back. But he can't help himself because he loves her and she's his heart and without her how will it beat? In his eyes is his soul, all that he has. He knows it would be enough if he could just reach up and touch her cheek.

"Don't look at me like that," she cries blowing her nose now. She looks from one eye to the other. "That look ... " Then her face becomes expressionless though tears still drip, like she's studying him, like after they first kissed. Like she's thinking if his head is enough to keep her feet from walking.

Pulling like taffy, he looks away knowing the break will give her enough limp candy between them to reach the door.

Face crumbling, she turns her back to him, shoulders shaking. He's like a church bell, hanging, steady, his gong heavy, weighing him down, knowing it'll be still. That she'll never ring it again.

She turns to look at him, tears just running down her face. So many her eyelashes stick together in points reminding him of the girl in his dreams under the falls. "I love you, Mike," she whispers.

His face is hard now with the metal around it that tears can't penetrate. He can't give her soft, he can't give her soft.

She backs up with small steps to the door, her eyes glistening with love 'til she blinks and he thinks the love is covered by relief.

"Goodbye," she holds her hand to her mouth as if to blow him a kiss, but she just drops it and grabs her coat and gloves and without putting them on, she's gone. Just like that, she's gone. Like Grace in his dreams who disappears when morning comes.

Left behind is a whisper. Of who she was in the room. Of what they were together. A silent sound he'll never hear again. Jenna's silent sound. Her music between his notes.

When the car pulls away, he doesn't feel the break. He's in the box. He pulls the lid down tight so mom won't know anything when she comes in to shut the light.

CHAPTER 35

April

Tommy's sitting in the leather chair watching the news. Mike's eyes are on the set but his mind is somewhere in the back of his head, replaying what happened a couple of weeks ago when Jenna left. Hasn't been able to shake it. Keeps rolling back and forth, going this way and that, thinking how things could have been different if he had said something different. Couldn't *do* anything different, but if he said something.

Should've been positive about how it could've worked rather than negative about the pain and stuff and how he wanted to end it. He'd told her what he talked to Joe and Tommy about, never thinking it might lodge a thought in her head that he would do it if they were together. Hell, he hadn't thought about anything in months except her. Even the pain seemed to take a back seat to his feelings—emotions that took over his body and made him feel full when he looked in her eyes. Should've done things different. Should've done things.

"What's that?" Tommy points to the TV.

Mike focuses, seeing the same old box of moving light that changes pictures behind glass. On the screen is a red car—shiny—with a man in a suit next to it. "The car?"

"No, that. The bag," he's pointing to a bag on top of the TV. There's a thin bag laying flat and Mike recognizes it as the brown bag Jenna left the night she brought the Slurpee. Mike thinks his eyes must have been cloudy from looking in the back of his head 'cause he hasn't seen it sitting there.

"Jenna left it."

Tommy turns sharply, eyebrows up. "What is it?"

"I don't know. Something from 7/11 probably." Remembered the edgy feeling inside when she said she called Nick. Mom moved the tray that night with the bag on it. She probably thought Jenna was coming back for it. He didn't ask her to open it 'cause he was steamed. Then he forgot about it.

"Let's see," Tommy gets up and brings it over. Turns it this way and that in his hand, mouth turned down, trying to feel what's in it.

"Ok?" Tommy asks before he puts his hand in the bag. Mike doesn't say anything to stop him.

Another book. A hardcover, a little bigger than the red one, but thin. About the size of a piece of toast. Tommy shows the cover—oriental type flowers overlapping the outline of a woman's face. On top is printed:

TO STUDY THE WAY IS TO STUDY THE SELF
TO STUDY THE SELF IS TO FORGET THE SELF
TO FORGET THE SELF IS TO BE AWAKENED.

-Dogen

"Whatever," Mike says.

Tommy flips it open but it's one of those books that doesn't stay open easily. Doesn't lay flat. Tommy presses it open and turns it to Mike, his fingers overlapping Jenna's handwriting that fills the page.

"Want me to read it?" Tommy asks.

"No, go get mom's stand so I can read." Mom has a cookbook holder that they use on the rare occasion that Mike reads. Still needs someone to turn the page so he doesn't read often.

Tommy comes back, puts the book on the stand and pulls the tray close. Seeing her handwriting in front of his face is like having her here. He can almost smell watermelon. He swallows a lump and begins reading while

Tommy sits down to watch the sports report. Joe would never sit; he'd hang over him wanting to know what she said.

Dear Mike,

If I could write music, I would write your story. I'd use a piano to describe your smile, a violin to describe your kiss, and the bittersweet sounds of a cello to play your heart.

Chords in perfect harmony would describe how I feel you inside me, [Yea, right, he thinks,] *how together we blend into a perfect song only you and I can hear.*

Like lightning on soft ground, your fire ignites a crescendo inside me with so many intricate notes it hurts my hands to play. I wish you could feel when I touch

"Hey, Tommy, turn the page." He does, then sits down. There's writing on both sides now.

your hand. I wish I could describe how your body moves, graceful and slow though you're still. How light comes through your eyes like a kaleidoscope bringing fun, laughter, and love, even with the pain mixed in. How we make love though we only kiss. How you touch my heart like no one else on earth.

What music would portray a man whose stillness creates movement, whose words drop in a silent lake and ripple until the lake is an ocean? It is music I will always hear and music I will play when my heart is lonely. I'll play it, hoping you can hear.

The strings from my heart to yours will always be there, even when you're in one place and I'm in another.

I want our hearts to meet again, somewhere in time, but for now

"Tom."

Tommy stands and turns the page, but it's blank. Turns another page. "Nothing else," Tommy says.

"Has to be," Mike's frowning thinking of the unfinished sentence. "Go back a minute." Tommy turns back to the writing. Mike reads the last line. Ends without a period. "...but for now ..." Did she mean to end it there? "Is there anything in back?" Mike asks. Tommy ruffles the pages. Shakes his head.

Mike's mind is racing. She came here that night to break up with him. Why else would she write that and bring it in here? Meant to give it to me. But she didn't finish. Or maybe she did. Maybe she was writing it in the car. Bought it at 7/11 and then wrote it in the car with the door light on. A hurried note to end it after all they had together? He's trying to remember being with her and talking and sharing deep thoughts and love, and he can't imagine she meant to leave it here. Maybe she was writing to herself. She wouldn't give him a journal. He can't write.

"What did she say?" Tommy asks.

Mike's eyes go to Tommy but his mind's mixed up thinking he should call her. But no, they ended it. He ended it. Thought he ended it to give her freedom. To go back to Nick or whoever. To find happiness. To live a normal life. Swallows. Throat is dry. "Gimme some," motions to his cup. Tommy holds it up for him, the book in his other hand. Mike takes three long sips. Doesn't feel it going down. Doesn't have the same satisfying fullness. Feels shallow inside like he might burp.

"Rip out the pages," he says to Tommy.

"What?"

"Rip 'em out."

Tommy just looks at him.

"Do it!"

Tommy opens the book and takes the written pages in one hand and pulls down. Mike sees the tattered ends left in the binding. "Tear 'em up. Little pieces and put 'em in the bag. Then throw it out. Outside where mom and Joe can't see."

"Don't you want to keep it? Read it over?"

"Just do it," Mike's eyes smolder.

"What did she say?"

"Nothing. We're done." Turns his eyes away to get back in the box. Pulls the lid down. Only now, he's not going to be searching in the back of his head anymore looking for answers. There's only one answer. And the way there is long. And he can't do it alone. He watches Tommy's strong, capable hands tear up the sheets, put them in the bag and roll the bag in a tight twist. Watches as he goes outside and comes back empty handed. Joe would never have done it. Joe would have read it and discussed over and over and maybe convinced Mike to call her. Maybe Joe should have read it. But no, he can't call. Every day he wants to call. Every night his heart longs to hear her voice, to smell her skin, to feel her kiss. But he's white now like the ceiling. Blank and absorbing what comes at him. Tommy lets him be white.

Tommy's standing next to the bed. "You're all pale."

"Yea."

"Maybe you should call her," Tommy says.

Mike looks up sharply, "You goin' "Joe" on me now?"

"What?"

"Never mind. Nothin'. Let me be."

Tommy sits down but he's shaking his head.

Gotta calm down, Mike thinks, gotta play this right. Glances at Tommy. Gotta play this right.

CHAPTER 36

1988

He's riding in the passenger seat of Tommy's Datsun 280Z. Tom's driving fast. The car has a T-top, where you take the sides of the roof off leaving a strip down the middle. The wind blows Mike's hair, but his aviators protect his eyes.

Strapped in, his seat is leaning way back. Now there's a shoulder strap for his bucket seat, not like mom's station wagon. He glances at the speedometer—80— then looks at Tommy's profile and his hands thumping the steering wheel in time to the music. Allman Brothers, *Jessica*, the instrumental that flies, is blasting. The music makes you want to run next to it. Tom's doing it with the car.

"Slow down, man. Gonna kill us." Mike yells over the wind.

"So?" Tom looks over a big smile on his face. He's 26 and still a kid in some ways. Works hard, plays hard. They're on their way down the shore to stay with friends, guys Joe doesn't like. Gave Tom a hard time.

"It's not a good idea," Joe had said standing on one side of the bed, Tommy on the other.

"What's the big deal? He's 32 years old," Tommy motioned toward Mike, not looking at him, Joe and Tom talking across him as if he wasn't there, like they did when he wanted to take Jenna to the drive-in.

"Those guys do coke," Joe said.

"Everybody does coke," Tommy said.

"Well, we don't."

"It's just a party!"

"Hold on, hold on," Mike said. "No one's doin' coke. We're just goin' down the shore for a weekend is all."

"I don't like it. Why not rent a place? We'll all go. Why do you have to go with these guys?" Joe's motioning with his hands as if he's Italian. Looks old to Mike, like he's got the weight of a six foot three inch man on his shoulders.

"Oh, that's fun—traveling with the family—mom and the kids. He's a grown man for Chrissakes. There's a party down there." Tommy's idea is to jumpstart Mike out of his two year doldrums and back to life. Been a couple of years now since Jenna, but the funk Mike's been in since is like a shallow grave. He's laying in it near the surface, can breathe and talk and all, but with his wasted legs, he can't climb out. And his brothers, mom, and sisters, well, they try, but they can't reach down far enough to pull him out.

"Joe, what's the big deal?" Mike asked knowing Joe's instincts are usually right.

"Remember the party way back when, when you smoked a joint? Right here in this room?" Joe pointed to the floor.

Mike remembered the girl on the rocks. Who he still dreamed of. "Yea," he smiled a crooked smile and glanced at Tommy.

"It's that asshole who gave you the pot whose house you're goin' to," Joe's lips are thin, pulled together. With all his responsibility, wife, kids, house, job, and quad, Mike understood the thin lips.

"I don't remember," Tommy said.

"Of course not, you were hardly born."

"It wasn't that long ago," Mike said.

"Who cares?" Tommy said, "That guy's older now too. Probably married and stuff like you," pointed to Joe.

"Calm down, calm down," Mike said. "I just want to go to the beach. Want to feel a little sand on my wheels." That stopped them in their tracks. They looked at him, faces blank, their circuits probably on full tilt remembering he's a man. That he's not a kid and they're not his parents. After a beat, they all laughed and Joe's lips relaxed knowing Mike can take care of himself even though he can't move.

Now speeding down the Atlantic City Expressway, Mike yells, "Gonna get a ticket."

"Great song," Tommy keeps thumping. "Gotta roll the wheels in time to the music."

Mike gets it. Understands the beat of music with tires rolling under you. Wishes the speed of the car would go faster and faster till they rise in the sky like a jet and fly out over the ocean. Maybe that's where I'll be someday, he thinks, relaxing back in the seat, enjoying the speed. Maybe I'll fly over the ocean with the salty air holding me up.

Looks at Tommy's hands thumping, thumping, but steady on the wheel. He'll need those hands. To get to the beach. He looks up through the open roof to the sky. It's wide and blue and filled with sun. When the time's right, he thinks, when the time's right. He closes his eyes.

CHAPTER 37

1989

Sun burns hot on the field and the players sweat in their red caps. Sounds of the crowd are muffled behind the glass of the air conditioned box. Mike prefers the outside seats where cheers and clapping make him feel one with the crowd, part of a group gathered for one purpose—to see the Phillies win.

Vet Stadium brings memories of when he played in the Catholic League championship football game during his junior year at Bishop Tremont. They won, of course, beating Archbishop Kendall.

He thinks about high school a lot lately. In the long hours of his nights, now that he doesn't sleep well (not telling Joe or Tom 'cause he doesn't want a pill), he wonders if he stayed at Tremont whether he'd be in this chair. Never got to college anyway. He thinks about why he changed schools and knew he had to do it because he could never have been sidelined wearing his uniform and crew cut, all revved up to get on the field. Could never have done that. And he can't do it now. He can't watch from the sidelines as everyone else lives life. Whatever seed lived in him back then to grow this gnarled tree, it's still inside. And he'll use it again, to jump out of his skin.

Watching the pitcher, he remembers all the times he practiced the moves. Precise, fine movements of the wrist and fingers honed to win. Maybe Dad was right and he should have stuck with baseball. Maybe he'd be on the mound right now, a pro, Dad and everyone in the stands cheering. But baseball never drove him the way football did. Or maybe it was Dad's smoldering eyes. Whatever it was, his choices drove him down this path on wheels.

Scenarios play in his head often now that the accident's 16 years back and people who knew him then are 16 years ahead with families and all. His chair can't keep up. His family can't push fast enough for where he wants to go.

A loud crack pierces the air from TV's that are hanging on the wall. Mike sees the live ball sailing into the stands. Von Hayes hit with enough steam to bring two guys home. The crowd rises, a sea of red, reminding him of another stadium long ago. The colors reflect on the clubhouse window like they did in the ambulance. Doesn't know why these old thoughts are in his head. Maybe because he's cut everything else out of his life. Drained it to the last drop. He dwells on the past, but doesn't talk about it. No one wants to hear old stories, not even Joe and Tom, who are hard to drain out of his life 'cause they are his life. But he's got to dry them up fast so he can pull himself from the living well of his family.

Joe and Tommy are celebrating, high fiving, beer spilling. It's a playoff game and Mike smiles, nods, pretends to be excited. Tries to get in the swing and let the crowd's jubilation wash over and refresh him. But he's stale inside.

Keeps up appearances for his family, though. Can't bring them down with him. They're always there for him. They've done so much. Always assure him they'll be there no matter what. Except the 'no matter what' doesn't include helping him die.

Whenever he brings it up, Joe says things like, "There's a reason for everything," or "We're managing the pain best we can," or "Hang on ... there might be a cure," or the worst thing he could say, "Don't know what I'd do without my kid brother," his eyes turning all glassy.

But the emptiness inside is a bottomless pit that his family's love and support can't fill. Wants a connection to fill the space. Not a connection like this crowd, all happy here in the stands and then fighting in the parking lot. He wants a skin dissolving on skin kind of connection, like he had with Jenna. And the only way there is through death.

As the crowd settles down and Joe gets him another beer, Mike smiles with a secret, a dark secret, but it makes his face lighter when he thinks of it. Joe laughs and his face brightens when he sees Mike's face open up like it used to. Joe's probably thinking he's in the moment of the game, enjoying his time here. That he's getting his spirit back. Maybe thinking they are through the worst of it. What Joe doesn't know is, he *is* through the worst of it. That he no longer has to think about ways to die—asking someone to feed him pills or hold a pillow over his head, or pour Draino in a cup and hold it to his lips. What Joe doesn't know is, yesterday he found a way.

While mom got lunch ready, Mike had asked her to turn on the TV so he could watch the news. Wanted to see the scores. But the top story is what caught his interest. A story of lost causes like him getting help from a doctor in Michigan—a doctor named Kevorkian.

His eyes had popped when he first saw the clip of a man in a bed, like him, consenting to the doctor tying a string around his hand, a string he could pull to release a poison to end his own life. Mike's stomach turned at first. Like a fist through it. He was horrified seeing the man's family there crying. Knew in that moment he'd never have people there. That he'd go it alone. Realizing he was already thinking how, his stomach settled with the satisfaction of control. Now there's a way. And he can decide whether to live or die. Didn't have to beg or plead. Only needed one thing—to get to Michigan to pull the string.

When mom brought in his lunch tray, the clip was over and they were reporting the weather. Mike's solemn eyes were back in, his face neutral so she wouldn't see he had streamers in his head, colored twists of crinkled paper filling the room all set for a party.

When mom went upstairs after lunch, he got a call. From Mary. At first he was happy to hear her voice but she was too polite, a little hesitant. Then, as if she was in Church, she whispered the reason for her call. In quiet tones she prepared him for what he knew was bad news when she said, "I have something to tell you."

That something was Jenna getting married. Next weekend. Jenna and Nick Stefano. Together forever.

After she said it, Mike had tried to sound happy, his voice higher than normal, asking Mary to give Jenna his best. When he hung up, he knew that Mary knew, that maybe Jenna had confided what happened between them. Maybe Jenna still cared, but she was marrying Nick.

The streamers in his head fell limp after he heard the news, his eyes stony like they had been, so no one noticed anything different. Didn't know he had ridden a roller coaster in the span of a few hours—the highest high, the lowest low, with the high being one that should have been a low, except after 16 years in bed.

Yesterday, he'd kept everything to himself—Kevorkian, Jenna, everything. He needed time to consider it now that death is a reality. Didn't want drama, everyone panicking, diving in and analyzing. Needed time to think. Wanted a clear road to his grave. Didn't want to muck it up with regret or confusion that he was doing it 'cause of Jenna. Timing is just coincidence, is all. Just because he saw the possibility of death one second before his life's possibility ended, it didn't mean he was dying because of Jenna.

So, he kept the news of her locked in his heart. Kept it to himself. A secret. One he'd take to the grave. And now he was going 'cause today when he asked, Tommy said he'd help.

CHAPTER 38

Mom cleans with the door open today. Dad's not home. Mike doesn't think of him anymore really. Hell, the Dad he knew from long ago, the thoughtful coach and teacher, are glimpses of a dead man. This Dad, who ever he is, Mike thinks of as just a boarder—someone who lives in mom's house.

No music today. Mom rarely listens to the radio anymore. Said she can't hear over the vacuum, but really she just wants to hear Mike, if he ever answers her steady stream of conversation. She talks to him now, her voice fading when she's straining, like when she reaches up or bends down. Mike can't hear much of what she says. Whatever it is, Mike knows she keeps it light. Doesn't say anything that will strike him deep. She probably knows, or maybe Joe told her, not to dig, not to probe to find out what Mike is really thinking.

A darkness lives on his face now, a shadow that grew after Jenna left, like there's no light in him. It lifts sometimes when Tommy brings friends over or when he goes out. Tommy always has one scheme or another to get his attention. Mike stopped doing the fundraising and event planning. Couldn't take the exertion. Felt like an old man. Just a guy in a shell, living life through his family's hands, without enough energy to pull them through his ordeal. He wants to let go, let them go. He wants to die. Tommy's helping, but there's twists and turns to work through.

"Your brother is coming this weekend for a cook-out," mom says from the kitchen. Her voice is muffled, a little ragged. Hears glasses clinking.

He pictures her taking the glasses, one at a time, from the dishwasher to the cupboard. Her thin hands wrinkled with the wear of care. Hands so familiar to him. Hands he loved and wished he could help.

She's telling him now what time they'd eat, the menu, who else would come. Mike assumes Dad won't be here.

"Hey mom?"

Everything stops. Her droning conversation, the clinking. Sees her with a glass mid-air, head turned, eyes sharp asking herself, "Did he say something?"

"Mom?"

The glass crashes. "What, Mike, what?" she's running.

"I'm ok, mom. I'm ok," he yells. As she comes in the room eyes scrambling, he thinks how sad it is that a glass breaks 'cause he called her.

"What is it, Mike?"

"I'm ok. Everything is ok. Calm down."

"Well, my oh my, you scared me yelling out like that!" she says, her hand to her chest.

"Sorry," he laughs. "It's gotten that bad, huh?"

Her eyes lighten with relief when she sees him smile. Her concern, her readiness to jump at his every whim, brings a sadness over him. A wet blanket sopped with tears, hers, his, tears of the ages. Lately, he isn't even thirsty 'cause he's filled up, almost drowning.

"Mom," his voice wavers and with the glass breaking and him drowning, he can't help but cry. She does too, holding his head close to her chest, her sobs in his ear coming through her heart.

She knows. He doesn't have to say. They both know the only answer to sitting in this bed is not her steady stream of conversation every morning. Her love is not enough to keep him grounded. He wants to fly, like in the jet to Lourdes. Wants a wind under his arms to carry him to where he can move again. Where he can dance and walk and run. It's not here. Will never be here. No matter what she and his brothers do. He's got to be free.

They all know now what he saw on TV—the magic of a stranger who will help. A man who will release them from their laden paths. They need time to adjust to the idea knowing it can happen. Will happen. What they don't know is that later today, Tommy is going to help him make the first phone call. To the lawyer. To set things up. So he can fly.

CHAPTER 39

1991

When it's time for leavin' I hope you understand.

Allman Brothers

Took two years to get plans in place. Calls, discussions, tears, heartache, family not really believing he would do it. Took turns listening to him, helping him with preparations. Right now, the Doc is the hold up—there's legal issues that could take another year or so. Doc wants to make sure before Mike flies to Michigan that his case will hold up, that he had tried other options, that he was truly ready, that he could pull the string.

Judy and Rita listen with concern when he talks about it, but their crying sets him off so he jokes with them. Makes it seem like he isn't serious. Joe and Tommy, their hearts in a twist, tug on either side of the issue, Tommy taking steps to make it happen, Joe trying to pull him back.

Tommy takes the brunt of Joe's objections 'cause without him turning the wheels, Mike would never get to Michigan. Joe thinks he can throw off the timing, but Tommy, loyal soldier, quiet linesman, listens, then does what the quarterback says to do.

Love pours between the jokes, fights, sarcasm. Not sappy, hugging kind of love, but a love that holds fast between brothers. Men who can see each other. Men who accept the weak and strong of each other.

Mike usually finds a joke to end a conversation about his road to death to keep Joe guessing and to keep Tommy from falling apart. Once he said that Tom would have to tell the hotel clerk they needed a room 'cause he has girls coming for his pity-party brother. Tommy thought he was serious and asked Mike if he really wanted a girl before going to Michigan. The sincerity on his face when he asked it, the caring, no matter what, made Mike reach that hand from his eyes and touch Tommy softly, like a pat on the shoulder.

Sometimes on a Friday night when Joe stayed late, the three would have a couple of beers, blast the music and talk about Mike's last requests. What he'd eat for dinner the night before, a party maybe, but they couldn't tell anyone it's a farewell party—they'd just have music and dancing, like the old days. Mike laughs at the things they came up with, knowing he'd do none of them, that he just wanted one thing. An impossible thing. What's tied up in his heart, where the smell and touch of Jenna lived. He'd like to see her one more time, kiss, cry with her for a proper goodbye. Drown in her eyes.

But those eyes looked at someone else now—a husband—and Mike's sure the cut-off look he'd see would leave him cold and empty. So he'll take the warm memory of Jenna with him to his grave.

His brothers kind of knew he'd like to see her, but they never said. Mom knew but kept herself busy around him. Tried to not let him see what's inside her, except the times she couldn't hold it in and they'd cry together, not saying anything, just tears in a puddle.

Her face held the lines his didn't—lines of aging as you move through life, worry lines. His face held up, unlike the rest of him. Only small bags under his eyes over clean shaven cheeks, mom insisting. Mike let her shave him every morning, knowing it was time spent together she'd remember. Time he'd carry with him to the hotel.

She played his music now when she cleaned—102.7—the station that used to be Wibbage, top ten pop. Now it's the same music but it's called classic rock. Music that aged while he sat in bed. Oldies that didn't wrinkle or show worry lines. Crosby, Stills, Nash & Young, the Stones, Lennon—

him dead too now. Mike's a classic, like the rest of his generation who are older, but still strong enough to have their own station.

Maybe there's great music where he's going. Lennon's still alive in the minds and hearts of his fans. Maybe people will remember me too, Mike thinks. Hoped people besides his family will know that he lived.

Now they wait. Wait for the Doc to call. Tommy keeps a few vacation days held back to use on a moment's notice. Every day, after Mike's dressed and settled in bed and mom's inside with the den door open, while her voice meets his ears with its familiar tones, every day, while listening and not listening to what she says while the music plays low, every day, he stares at the phone. A low rumble in his gut like a freight train keeps him ready for when it will hit.

CHAPTER 40

1992

Dinner is quiet tonight. Just Mike and mom over a plate of meatloaf and mashed potatoes. Joe and Michelle took the kids down the shore so it's been a week since Joe was here. Mike missed the nonchalant way Joe made him feel like a regular guy, even when massaging his back or arms. Like he's at the Y getting ready to work out and Joe is the old guy who gets the athlete's muscles ready. When Joe isn't around, Mike feels paralyzed.

No music tonight. Mike asked mom for no stereo or TV. Wants to hear what's in his head—make sure it matches what's in his heart. They got the call about three months back, but then the Doc got tied up again in legal issues. So, it's back to the waiting game. When Joe's here talking and the music's blaring, Mike doesn't have to think as clearly 'cause Joe helps him see.

Tonight, his heart is soggy, wet with despair. Needs Joe's sounding board eyes, his careful but certain words to hit him in the chest, wring out his heart and keep it beating. Needs Joe as surely as he needs the meat and potatoes on the fork. That's why it's Tommy taking him to Michigan.

With Tommy, it's a different kind of bond. Mike sometimes thinks Tommy understands him more, knows him better without all the words that are between him and Joe. Tommy still looks up to him, even when he carries him like an infant.

"Did you see on the news today the big meeting of physicists that are in Philadelphia? It's in all the papers." Mom cuts another bite.

Mike chews. "What's it about?"

"Oh, they're reporting on advances in medicine, things like that."

"Oh."

Mom's always trying to get him interested again in the *hope* of medicine rather than using it the way he intends to use it.

"Rita called. She's coming later to drop off my Avon order."

"I'm done," Mike shakes his head when she offers the next forkful.

"You hardly ate anything!" Mom keeps the fork in mid-air.

"Arms hurt today. Don't feel right."

"Did Tommy give you your pill at lunch?"

Mike's eyes slide to mom's, not answering. His look says the pill doesn't matter, that the pain will always be there. That there's no way to get rid of it but through Tommy taking him.

She places the fork on the plate and pulls the tray next to her. Blood drains from her face, her freckles going from brown to gray. As surely as Joe and Tommy know him, she knew him more. The deeper answer in his eyes pulled life from hers, as if blankness is all she can handle, as if she is like the white ceiling, absorbing his black and white thoughts without any colorful answers.

"Tommy's taking me to Michigan, mom. You know that." His stomach churns the meatloaf, pushing it around till he feels sick.

Her lips pull tight making the white of her face whiter.

"What happens, Mike, tell me again ... what the doctor does ... I don't ... understand," her voice is soft, almost a whisper.

Watching her mouth form the words, not really moving, Mike knows not to tell all. They had decided to keep the details from her and she let them, but now she's asking. "He gives me medicine, mom, through a tube. But I pull to open the valve." He motions with his left arm, the slight motion everyone cheered about 19 years ago.

There, he'd said it. Told the woman who gave him life and who kept him alive all these years that he could pull a string to end it. Wondered if she thought he'd ended it at the dinner table so long ago when he'd said he was switching schools to play at Washington.

Covering her mouth, her eyes glisten but no tears fall, absorbing what he has to say. Then, lowering her hands, she clasps them tightly in her lap as if she has to hold on to herself.

"You're a man who can make his own decisions. But don't do it because you think you're a burden to me, your brothers or sisters." One tear drops wetting her blouse, belying her matter-of-fact voice.

"Mom, we've been through this."

"I just want to say it," she looks at him.

In her eyes he sees love, that unconditional, proud, mother type of love. Remembers the look in Dad's eyes so long ago. He wonders if she and Dad talk about him. He wonders who they'll be without him between them.

"It's because I'll never carry my own burdens, mom. I played in the game and now you guys carry everything for me."

Standing abruptly, she hits the tray and it topples, crashing the dish to the floor. She doesn't even look in the direction of the shattered glass. Just grabs and holds him. Mike's eyes widen remembering another time when glass broke and she held him to her chest. Sobs wrack her body, him unable to hold or comfort her with other than his words, which he can't say 'cause he's being carried on an ocean, a wave he started that there's no way to stop except when it collides on the beach.

Knowing he's the source of her crying, that he did this to her, that her days will soon be her own, no more meals to cook and feed him, wondering if she'd clean with the radio on or off and who she'd talk to with the house so quiet, the sadness that he carries bursts through and his sobs match hers, a bundle of tears falling down on the bib, soaking through to his already drenched heart.

CHAPTER 41

Monday Night Football used to be a big party in Mike's room. Not anymore. Even for a big game like tonight—Eagles vs. Giants, the heated rivalry being played in the Meadowlands in north Jersey, the neutral state bridging New York and Philly.

Almost as if planned, Joe comes alone. Mike didn't think it was unusual for Joe to be here without his friends, but he knew something was up when Tommy called to say he had a conflict, that he couldn't be here to watch the game. That didn't ring true and when Joe came in with the six pack and chips, Mike just followed him with his eyes, waiting for a show down.

Sitting in the leather chair where Tommy usually sits, Joe munched, drank and kept his eyes on the screen, making occasional remarks about the plays, not jumping up and down like Tommy. The phone loomed on the tray Joe pushed over near the stereo, as far away from Mike as he could get it.

A quiet first-half with the Giants leading 3 – 0 makes the room seem emptier, Mike missing Tommy's antics. Maybe Joe and Tommy had a fight, Mike thinks, his eyes cutting to Joe to see what he could read on his face. It's possible with everything going on. Mike's sure there are behind the scenes talks and can hear angry words being thrown about, Joe's, Tom's and mom's. Probably the girls too, but mostly, they stayed out of it. Joe's still trying to get Mike to change his mind.

On the screen, the announcers review Sunday's games showing replays. Mike's not interested. His eyes are tired and football is black and white in his head, knowing yards aren't important, steps are. Steps he can't take except to get to Michigan.

"Want anything?" Joe's voice cuts through his thoughts.

Mike shakes his head no.

Joe gets up and when he opens the door, Mike hears the game on in the den. With the door open, Mike hears Joe say something to Dad. Hears a mumbled answer. Been so long since he heard his voice. Wonders what he looks like now. Tries to picture him, but all he can see is a young man with hard eyes. Probably gray and fat now, Mike thinks. Memories of him drained from his mind long ago, sometimes forgetting he lived in the same house, not noticing when he came or went like he used to. Dad's absence or presence is another pain Mike had learned to hold level inside like a slow burn simmered to gray ash, wispy and deadened. With the den door open, Mike wants to spark the embers, call out, start a fight, see if anything runs hot or cold. But he hasn't in all these years and he won't now.

Plate in one hand mustard in the other, Joe's got soft pretzels. Five connected together, thin and salty. He closes the door behind him.

"Someone went to center city today," he says, eyes bright. Placing the dish on the bedside table, he pours yellow mustard in wavy lines over the five. Breaking one off, he takes the end and eats it, offering Mike the soft middle bite. "Good!" Mike says chewing.

"They don't have this in NY!" Joe says, holding it up to the TV. "Morons," he adds, lowering the volume and turning the chair to face Mike.

Here we go, Mike thinks.

After biting more pretzel, Mike motions with his chin to the beer. Joe gives him a drink and sits down. Mike decides to do what's natural. Goes on offense.

"How much longer can you do this anyway? Feed me pretzels and beer?" he asks as if he's picking up a conversation they just left off.

"As long as it takes," Joe says, chewing and looking at the pretzel, not at Mike. The edge in his voice tells Mike he's pissed. "You and Tom got this all figured out, don't you?" He licks mustard from his fingers.

"It's the only way, man."

"So, you call the shots, not thinking of anyone else, what matters to anyone else," Joe's eyes flash then go back to the pretzel.

So, that's it, Mike thinks. Joe's back on how Mike's death will affect him, mom, the family. Maybe he's not sure who he'll be without his visits here every day.

"Think I like this pain I sit in every day? I just don't talk about it much anymore. We've been down this road, Joe. A thousand times we've been down this road." Joe's picking salt off his lap.

"Look at me," Mike says and Joe looks up. "You never thought I'd do it," Mike's voice is flat.

"Actually ..." Joe drops his eyes, "I never thought you'd do it without me."

And Mike's heart squeezed. He wishes he could touch Joe's arm, relieve him of his duty, thank him. "Joe ... you're my life, man. Without you I wouldn't have one. I can't ask you to keep me alive anymore. And I don't need your help to die."

"I'm your brother!" Joe sits forward in the chair. "I'm the one who played ball with you and took you everywhere and stood at all your games. Not Tommy! And, as far as keeping you alive, I don't do anything I don't want to do."

"I hear you, man, and you are my brother. Not my mother, or nurse-maid, or father ..." Mike didn't know where that came from. Sometimes he thought of Joe like a dad, a real dad, one who cared. Their eyes held.

"Don't put me in with him," Joe says shaking his head.

Mike dropped his head back on the pillow wanting to close his eyes but instead rested them on the ceiling. His old friend dancing with gray shadows from the TV.

"I'm tired, man."

Joe stands, "Don't do this, Mike. Leave it awhile, let it sit. You don't know what will happen down the road."

It hurt Mike to see the pain in Joe's eyes, like a lonely wind on an empty beach with nowhere to go.

"I gotta go," Mike says, "Gotta get out of this bed."

"Stay with me and Michelle for a week or two, see how you feel after that. The kids will love it!" Joe smiles.

There he goes again. Knowing what to say to keep Mike grounded. In his mind's eye he sees Joe's home full of love and warmth, sees them sitting around the TV in the living room as a family, Mike included. Knew Michelle would love for him to stay. She'd set up Backgammon and they'd play, with her moving his chips of course, even when he puts her back. Love filled the rooms in Joe's house, like Mike imagined his house would be—wife, kids, friends, fun.

It tempted him. The pull of Joe's life and Joe willing to share it brings a warmth inside. But all the fuss, the arrangements to get him there, him being a one man circus act needing all the set-ups to perform, after all that, he knows the love there can't fill what's empty inside. Might drain him more with thoughts of what could've been. And if he's at Joe's, who will be here to answer the phone?

"Thanks, man," he says looking at Joe, the other side of him, living half there, half in the bed. Sees his reflection in Joe's eyes—the tall guy on the field with a ball in his hand. Joe doesn't see the lump in the bed, doesn't feel the dead weight of him. Just sees the athlete, the brother he ran and played with, who he'd stand by for years to come.

Mike raises his arm and Joe takes his hand. Mike sees a single tear run down Joe's cheek, the period on a conversation they started so long ago.

CHAPTER 42

March, 1993

I will sing this victory song. 'Cause I'm already gone.

Eagles

Rita, Judy, mom, and Tommy eat dinner in Mike's room. Well, they don't really eat; just bring food to their mouths and chew. The last supper, Mike thinks, being fed his favorite—mom's roasted chicken. It sticks in his throat but he pushes it down, not wanting to hurt her anymore than he already has, though not eating her chicken and going off to die can't really compare.

Earlier when Joe was here, Mike didn't tell him tomorrow's the day. Mike wanted to keep what's between them strong and carry it with him to Michigan. After Joe's car pulled away, Mike drowned in tears. Tommy cleaned him up good before mom came in with the tray. The girls (now women but he still thought of them as girls), came in behind her with dishes, silverware, and flowers.

His sisters are sleeping here tonight to be with mom after he leaves tomorrow morning. Wonders if Dad thinks the dinner is a party or if they'd told him.

This morning Mike had asked for egg salad, figuring it was a special day, his last. But he couldn't look at mom when she placed the dish in front of him. Didn't want her to see the surprise in his eyes when he saw the green yolks. He just ate, knowing her eyes didn't see the green, just saw him all daffodil yellow, not dried up in his middle like the eggs. She was so focused on him she didn't hear the eggs screaming they were done.

After the dinner plates are cleared, the four gather 'round the bed and bend their heads in prayer. They talk in soft whispers like he's sick and resting. Like they would if he had cancer or something and it's his last hour. Like something changed in him and they couldn't blast music and laugh and talk like they did all these years. It's a reverence, the whispering. A stepping back in respect for a man who soon will be dead. Guess I'm in hospice, he thinks.

Mike's eyes glaze as the girls say goodnight and leave the room with tissues pressed to their faces. Doesn't want to think of the last of anything. Mom is next. She leans over, caresses his cheek and tells him to call her if he's awake and needs anything. Asks if he wants her to sleep on the cot and he mumbles no.

Mom's eyes are dry and clear, like she can see his freedom, his spirit breaking free from suffering. He knows that she knows he cares about what's in her heart but his freedom is more important. Her Catholic is out in spades. Whispers that the Blessed Mother will take care of him, that she's prayed to her and knows she'll be there. Mike hopes she's right and leans into her eyes to take a little of her faith with him.

Tommy's quiet. Doesn't say much, just offers the sleeping pill and water. Mike takes it wishing they could leave now and he didn't have to go through another night and another set of goodbyes in the morning.

After Tommy goes upstairs and the house is quiet, Mike turns to the window. It's cold and dark. This time tomorrow, he'll be dead. Well, he'll be somewhere.

Thinking of the saints and angels that he learned about in school, he wonders if he'll see them. Wonders if he'll be able to see his empty room, empty bed, finally free from the four walls. Or will he be in the arms of the Lady as mom said? Maybe he'll seek comfort from his tired journey and rest his head on her lap like a child.

But none of the options ring true. What he pictures is the ocean, rocks jutting into the sea, him standing on the jetty with strong, sure legs, feeling the thunder of the waves in them again. When he pictures it, he's alone.

Jenna's face appears in his mind. He thought to call her—all this week, and last, and the one before that. But she's long married. Probably has kids. He didn't know; never asked. All those good feelings that lived inside him when she was here, all the things they shared, were locked in a pocket of his heart where no one could see. His secret. The only thing he kept hidden from Joe. Most times, he hid it from himself.

Turning to the ceiling, he pushes his head back in the pillow. I can only take with me what's inside, he thinks. Doesn't really know, though. Doesn't know anything, where he'll be, what will happen when he dies. Only thing he knows is he won't be here. Won't be in a bed staring at a ceiling unable to get out. Waiting for someone to feed him, change him, give him a drink. No more waiting. Just until morning.

CHAPTER 43

Michigan

I'm alive, I breathe the air, wash the earth from my face.

Sammy Hagar

"Can I say something?" Mike asks, glancing from the doctor to the camera. The doctor is focused on pouring liquid into the pouch.

"Of course," the doctor says still working.

"Doc ... Doc," The doctor turns, finished with pouring, looking Mike straight in the face. "I want to say thank you ... thank you for helping me. I'm grateful ..." he pauses smiling, "I'm grateful you're in the world ... to help me." Mike laughs in his mind thinking of all the times Joe said to be grateful. Through all the pain and all of his heartache, here he is, finally grateful.

Smiling, the doctor's face brightens. "It's my purpose. I feel it's my purpose. We all have one, you know." He goes back to work sealing the top of the pouch.

"So, am I part of your purpose?" Mike asks, no edge in his voice, just a question at the end of his life.

"No, no, son. My purpose is to allow you your freedom to choose how to live. Or die," he points to the pole standing at attention holding the liquid now poised and ready for action. "You must have fulfilled your purpose otherwise you would not be here with me now," he says, opening both arms, palms raised to the ceiling, as if to encompass all that is contained in the room—the unemotional furniture, the pole, the camera, life, death.

"That's what Joe would say," and his eyes tear. The doc raises his eyebrows. "My brother. My older brother." And he thinks of Joe and Rita with only one younger brother now and Tommy and Judy with only one older brother. Thinks of the gap that will live in the family now. A big hole in the middle where before he took up all the space.

"The liquid is ready," the doctor says coming close to the bedside, glancing at Bill then back to Mike. A sickness rises in Mike, a creeping fear, threatening to stop him. To make him cry like a baby and run home to mom.

Doc places his hand over Mike's, over the string. "If you move this hand, your arm, the valve will release and the poison will enter your bloodstream causing your death. Do you understand?"

The sickness floods his head knowing he's gonna die. He's gonna do this and die. He locks on Doc's eyes to steady himself—gray flecked with green—and thinks what's behind those eyes could talk for miles. He feels the contact, the skin on skin, just by looking in this man's eyes. What he's seen, what he's done for people. What he's doing now for Mike. And the sickness fades, replaced by a thank you. A heartfelt thank you. And he sends it to the Doc as if he reached out and touched his arm.

"Yea, Doc, I got it." Still holding the Doc's eyes with his own, he whispers with a pang of bittersweet, "You're the man."

Doc frowns then nods, not really knowing that all of the respect and gratitude Mike has inside, for his family helping him live, for the doctor helping him die, are held in those words. Words his twelve year old brother said. Words that meant love.

Doc steps back from the pole. "Please say something, Mike. Just to show I did not open the valve."

Pausing, Mike looks at the camera. "I coulda been a contenda," he says in Marlon Brando lingo, a teasing smile on his face.

Doc chuckles, "Humor helps, humor helps. Take it with you, Mike."

This is it. Bye momjoetommyjennalife, he thinks. He pulls the string.

CHAPTER 44

Ceiling is the sky; you're the sun and as you shine on me, I feel free.

Cream

At first, nothing. Blinking, he turns his eyes to Doc, who looks on pensive and calm, as if the drip from the pouch Mike had just uncorked is normal, routine.

Mike watches the drips, each one bringing him a step closer to ... what? He wants to ask the doc but his mouth is tongue-tied, his jaw unable to open. Looking down at the hand with the string wrapped around it, he realizes that all the years of trying to move that hand, all the pain and effort, led him to this moment. It's why he trained, persisted, so he could have control. Free himself from misery. So he could choose. Like choosing to play, change schools, put on a red and white uniform, throw the ball.

A tingling inside his head makes his eyes droopy. Blinking at the ceiling, he doesn't want to see the corky holes with their arms outstretched. Prefers to think of the ocean so he closes his eyes and the tingling forms waves. Swirling, white, foamy, salty, all in his head like it's always been.

Then, his eyes spring open and the ceiling's back, a burst of white, blinding, caught in his chest, wanting to reach up and hold his fist to his heart, tear it out 'cause the pressure is killing him. But, like always, he can't move.

Grimacing, he closes his eyes and sees mom smiling through the swirls and the salt. He hears, "There, there," but it isn't mom's voice, it's a man. Dad! He looks through the mist, pushes it away to find Dad. "It won't be long, son." Son! He knows I'm here, came to get me—we didn't say good-bye, he came to say goodbye, he came to see me—wants to shout—but his mouth won't move and the mist is so warm, and the pain goes away when he's in it.

The air is fresh and charged with excitement. His face is wet with it. He wipes his face—feels the tears. He *feels* the tears! Palms in front of his face—his hands—they're wide and strong ... like Tommy's. "Look Dad!" And he turns to show him his hands, palms up, smiling, joy running through him from his head to his toes, bursting from the inside out—the hand from the wall opening its fist, as if he is the wall, he is the fist, he is his hand, and he holds it out to Dad, his mind making the movement, but his hand reaching out.

Dad's standing in a backdrop of white. But it's not young Dad, it's Dad as he must look now, older, with glasses and he's smiling and the warmth in his eyes locks in Mike's heart. And Mike knows. Knows now why Dad's eyes smoldered, why Dad sat immobile in the den, unwilling to come into Mike's room. It was so Mike would live. To give Mike the drive to prove to Dad he could live with his choice. The nubby callous that grew between them kept them apart, but kept Mike alive whether he moved or not. And in his knowing, the nub is gone, Dad's rejection is gone. And all that's left is love.

⌘ ⌘ ⌘

Wind on his face, arms outstretched, he holds the world. Salt sprays from the ocean in front of him stinging his face, refreshing, tingling his skin with time and depth. Waves burst in eternal movements—pushing forward, drawing back, each forward motion gathering steam for the next plunge, taking what it can from the sand, the sweet mixture of sun and salt.

The beach stretches for miles in either direction. An empty beach full of the taste and smells of life and the magic of death. Sand shifts beneath his feet. He looks down. *Sand shifts beneath his feet!* Balancing on soft mounds, he wiggles, pressing in deeper, the sand warm and soft , his feet wide and flat—*feet wide and flat*—not crumpled and useless. Without effort, his mind signals his feet to hold him upright. Balance, movement, again lived in him.

Reaching up to wipe his eyes, he realizes he's not wearing glasses. He feels the small wetness on his finger and his mind flashes to all the tears others wiped so he could see.

Water laps over his feet cooling them and flattening the sand. Tide's coming in, he thinks and bends over to roll up his pants. When he does, he notices his left sleeve is higher than his right and turns to see a small black and blue mark on the inside of his elbow. A cold room flashes in his mind and kind eyes behind big glasses and he's filled up with the decision of it, and he is glad.

Standing, he's ready to take a step. Not knowing how, not caring how, he thinks it and his foot steps forward. One foot, then the next—balanced, the magic inside to be used at his whim, his desire—like Tommy jumping out of his chair after a good play or bad.

Laughing, he kicks the water, playfully, happily, and the strength of two strong legs fills him with energy. "Joe! Mom!" he yells, then turns to his right and takes off in a sprint. In the wet sand, the sun overhead, the wind stings his body with joyful pleasure, and hits his eyes making him cry.

"I'm running!" he screams to the wind as tears roll down his cheeks, some reaching his lips, their taste bitter and sweet, like life. Others are brushed off by the force of his forward motion, his salt joining the salt of the sea, his small contribution to the whole, adding to the majesty of waves and changing tides. Arms pumping, strong athlete's legs propel him forward in this new life.

Running, his feet cut through water that could go on forever as long as he wants to keep moving, as long as the fire inside him fuels the motion of perfect harmony between arms and legs, muscles and bones in perfect symmetry to the music in his head.

Lost in the world of motion, his strong breathing matches the quick strides. Physical exertion is exhilarating after so long lost in bed. Nerve endings burst with the current of clear signals from his brain, from somewhere inside, his heart maybe, enjoying the forward motion, the speed of life.

A distant sound, familiar, comes from behind, a droning, monotonous sound getting louder and stronger till it's overhead. Glancing up, still running, it's a plane, a big one, low over his head, the shadow wafting over him like a big bird. Its rumble turns to music, a melody he remembers that lived in his heart.

Arms and legs pump harder to keep up with the shadow moving quickly over him, moving beyond him. Straining to keep up, he's sprinting, running full out, veins popping on his neck, arms in ninety degree angles up and down to move forward as if he's flying like the plane.

He runs like he did as a kid. Looking up, he sees the Pan Am insignia—the blue circle world—proudly displayed on the plane that took him to Lourdes. The tail is so close he sees the lines intersecting the blue circle, like the lines intersecting his travels on the blue earth. He sees his life there on the rudder, an instrument that with just one ounce of pressure can turn this magnificent jet, like one fissure in his spine turned him and changed the course of his life and the lives of others. And he understands.

Needing to catch up, wanting to go to the rocks and expel the mystery from them, the mystery that soaked in his soul, he has to catch the plane.

But his pumping arms and legs can't match its speed. The wind blowing past his ears creates a melody, a singing, a chorus of voices so beautiful the sound aches in his head and reaches down to squeeze his heart.

Closing his eyes, he slows his run and reaches his arms out like the wings, mimicking the plane's stance in the sky, the wind of a thousand butterflies rising inside.

Suddenly, his body grows bigger or the jet becomes smaller, because now he's looking down on it, he's above it and his shadow fills the shape of the plane. Somehow he is one with the immobile form whose purpose is to fly and carry. In the blending, he joins his wishes to his heart, his learning to his pain, his love and laughter. He knows his arms on earth carried the people who traveled with him; people who touched him and changed him from the inside out—his Mom, his brothers, Jenna. How, even though he couldn't move, he held them deep in his heart, their steam and motion combining with his strength to make him whole. And he is free.

EPILOGUE

As we sailed into the mystic.

Van Morrison

Quietly he walks next to high walls of white stone that surround the Garden blocking his view of the other side. The walls keep him focused on the lush greenery—flowers and smells that captivate. Music here is wistful and pure.

Following his usual path, he arrives at a small pond, where he often sits contemplating his future, his past. Benches near the water invite him to sit and stare into it, his eyes going as deep or as shallow as he wants, depending on how it reflects.

Sometimes the past shows soft ripples of love and family; sometimes he goes deeper and sees pain. But he doesn't feel it. He only sees the reflection of it and how it changed him.

On this day, sitting on the bench, he's restless. His insides churn like the ripples in the water, starting something where there is nothing, waves undulating in his head. With serenity shattered, he ignores the birds luring him to sit and ponder. Instead, he turns his head, a little ... to the left. Just there, beyond the wide trunk of a tall tree, is a path where the limbs of small trees join overhead. He knows to go there is a risk. He's been beckoned before. But he always turned his head back to the pond, preferring the nature sounds and the soft water to rest his soul. Today, he's curious.

Walking toward the tree, the birdsongs turn to music that's clearer, sharper in his head. Chirps turn into words. Words that mean something, meant something ... a man's voice ... *We were born before the wind* ... he keeps walking ... *Also younger than the sun* ... he ducks to avoid branches holding hands overhead.

Bare feet balance perfectly on the dirt path. There's an opening ahead, a divide in the wall where air flows through hitting his face. The smell of time, gravity, reminds him and pulls.

Let your soul and spirit fly into the mystic.

Garden air blends with air from the other side mixing what's inside his head and heart. *I want to rock your gypsy soul* ... notes like granules under his feet ... *Just like way back in the days of old* ... each one a nuance, each one important to sustain him on the path. Time on his skin beats in his heart. Thoughts gel as if they're tangible ... *And together we will float* ... as if he can touch them ... *into the mystic.*

 Getting lost inside his brain, distracted by music and time, he focuses to keep marching to the opening. Like pulling himself from a silky grave, one that held him because it had to, he knows now it is time to get through the wall.

Weaving his way, the opening appears to shrink as he gets closer, as if it will close before he reaches it. Hurrying, the music fades and the smell of humanity hits him in the face almost pushing his head back. But he knows he has to keep going.

Running now to catch the opening, the branches open overhead and he's under a black sky. The wall is retreating but he runs flat out like he did on the beach. His lungs are heavy with air and it hurts and feels good at the same time. His eyes sharpen on the opening, eyes not blocked by glasses or fear. And his intention is so clear that suddenly the opening is in front of him and he stops short, breathing hard, and looks up at the high walls of white with the narrow passage between them.

The white reminds him of the unreachable white of a ceiling. Like the one he passed through. The smell of the ocean hits his face, salty, stinging, and he knows he has to move.

Stepping into the long passage, he raises hands on both sides grazing them over the walls as he walks, the smooth surfaces warming him. Smells and sounds are heavier now. They seep into his bones as if he's caving in and it hurts his hands and feet, but he keeps going. He hears music again but it's louder and more distant at the same time, as if he is the music but he has to keep walking to hear the notes.

Watermelon—the sweet musical smell of watermelon—Jenna!—and he knows his course is clear. That he has to push to get to the other side.

His insides pull tight. Hands are no longer flat on the wall but are curling in on themselves, cramping, causing him to gasp, a sound he hasn't uttered in so long. A sound not needed in the honey air of the Garden. But this air, well, this air carries familiar tinges of pain that catch in his throat.

At last, he reaches the end of the passage. Behind him, a sucking sound like a vacuum closes the gap and the wall is smooth, impenetrable. But he's not frightened. He knows his thoughts can open the wall when he is ready.

In a stone courtyard, there's a walkway to his left. Stepping toward it, he loses his balance on gravel crunching under his feet. Leaning on the wall to make his way, the small stones hurt his feet. He thinks of the soft earth of the Garden. But he can't turn around. His head is too full of the smell of the earth—heavy, wistful, pure.

Bones weary, as if they'd lived a hundred years, pain creeps down his shoulders into his arms, cramping fingers. With labored breathing, he stumbles on, legs tired, mouth dry, thirsty, a craving to swallow the liquid ocean raging in his head, the need, the want, surprising him.

He can't walk anymore and leans against the wall. Hands in knots, he crosses his arms over his chest. He has to work fast or be stuck here unable to move. He has to reach Jenna and tell her.

The smell of life is strong—fruity, musky. Closing his eyes, he thinks of her hair, her smile, her eyes. Focusing on her eyes, he calls to her in her sleep. In this time-filled air, in this cold courtyard, bones hurting, he falls into her dream.

Their thoughts merge. Now she's standing with him in the courtyard. He's looking down at her. She's looking up, eyes filled with wonder and love. Inside him, happiness flows when he feels her touching him though she doesn't, except with her eyes. Like when he was with her once beneath the stars. And that's his message, what he has to explain before his legs give out. Before he can no longer hold her with his mind.

About to collapse, he bears down to keep his legs strong for her, for this moment to be shared, a moment he couldn't give her on earth. Speaking quickly, his voice is deep and strong like it used to be. A voice he hasn't heard in ... he didn't know. He tells her all that he knows, all that she knows, but doesn't remember. About life, death, things important and heartfelt and she takes it in with her eyes, smiling, nodding, understanding. Unlocking her weariness, he sees it replaced with courage and hope. And he knows his course is true. He knows he had to fight his way to the courtyard for this moment with Jenna, for her, for him, knowing he has to go back, that he reached her when he walked on the path through walls of stone.

He came to remind her of blessings and promises of the completeness of life. Of joining mind to body in oneness of purpose, of what she had yet to accomplish, locked in her head and her heart.

He came to remind her of their laughter and tears, each important to the knowing of what could exist between a man and a woman—what had to exist for her ... in her life.

She takes in his words, eyes luminous as she glances from his hands to his face, not saying anything, but he sees her happiness to see he is standing and he wants her to tell his brothers.

Pressure inside grows deeper and stronger, enough to crush him. Enough to keep him stuck here where he doesn't want to be, can't be. He leans over and presses his lips to her neck, deeply, lingering, her smell lifting him to a peak inside he remembers from before.

Then she's gone. His eyes water and the tears allow him to see down. Down through the black sky and the stars, like a shot of light piercing the universe. He looks down to the earth, falling, seeing, pinpointing a house, a bedroom, a woman—Jenna—deep in her bed, dreaming. He leans down and kisses her again.

She bolts upright, tears streaming down her face, hand on her heart, eyes wide. He sees her reach up to touch her neck where he kissed her. She sobs into bed sheets wiping her face, and his heart swells knowing he reached her on this first small journey, a journey he would make again, in time. Through time and space he reached her. Through thought and purpose, he reminded her.

And he remembered Grace, the woman who came to him in his dreams. Who made him feel things he couldn't feel. Who made him feel. Grace connected his mind to his body while he slept. It's what he hoped to do for Jenna.

And he knew she would tell his family he's ok, that he lived for a purpose. That what was supposed to happen, happened. That the people he touched and who touched him are what mattered, even though he couldn't touch. Jenna will tell them, he thinks, his insides now turning to stone.

Stumbling, he works his way back to the opening on stiff legs, with cramped arms and hands. Pebbles burn the bottom of his feet. Remembering endurance, he pushes through it like he did so many times before. He doesn't know how long it takes, but it doesn't matter. Time isn't the same here as it is on earth.

As he approaches the courtyard, a softness flows through him loosening his tied up limbs. Closer still, his arms unlock and relief flows through his mind and heart. The heaviness of gravity that pulled him to Jenna releases him and the opening appears at the edge of the passage.

He hears music. A melody without words—violins, sweet harps, an intricate crescendo. Jenna's music. And he wants to see her once more, to see if she remembered.

Stepping into the passage, half in, half out, he looks back to where he stood with Jenna. His heart fills up and tears sting his eyes. Through their glistening, his vision is clear, magnified, and he drops down again in his mind and sees Jenna sitting on a porch, her face serene. Chimes hang in open windows, and leaves on the trees whisper like a soft kiss.

Reaching further with his energy, he sends his heart and the music and the wind, the wind of his soul. His intention is so strong the chimes ring in the breeze. He sees her look up. A notebook is open on her lap, the pages blank. When the chimes ring again, a pen rolls from a table and lands on the floor. He smiles, wings on his heart, when she picks up the pen and begins to write.

APPENDIX

Lyric Permissions

1. CHAPTER 3, Pg. 9
SHOOTING STAR
Words and Music by PAUL RODGERS
(C) 1974 (Renewed) WB MUSIC CORP. and BADCO MUSIC, INC.
All Rights Administered by WB MUSIC CORP.
All Rights Reserved

2. CHAPTER 7, Pg. 29
LITTLE BIT O SOUL
By JOHN CARTER AND KENNETH HAWKER
(pka: Carter-Lewis)
Copyright 1965 by Carter-Lewis Music Pub.Co. Ltd.
Administered by PEERMUSIC III, LTD., in the United States
Used by permission. All rights reserved.

3.   CHAPTER 8, Pg. 35
GOOD MORNING STARSHINE (FROM "HAIR")
Music by GALT MacDERMOT Words by JAMES RADO and
GEROME RAGNI
© 1966, 1967, 1968, 1970 JAMES RADO, GEROME RAGNI,
GALT MACDERMOT, NAT SHAPIRO and EMI U CATALOG INC.
All Rights Administered by EMI U CATALOG INC. (Publishing) and
ALFRED MUSIC PUBLISHING CO., INC. (Print)
All Rights Reserved

4.   CHAPTER 9, Pg. 39
CARRY ME THROUGH
DON BREWER/CRAIG FROST
© 1976/1987 BREW MUSIC CO. (BMI)
Used By Permission
All Rights Reserved, International Copyright Secured

5.   CHAPTER 10, Pg. 43
RIVER
Words and Music by JONI MITCHELL
© 1971 (Renewed) CRAZY CROW MUSIC
All Rights Administered by SONY/ATV MUSIC PUBLISHING,
8 Music Square West, Nashville, TN 37203
All Rights Reserved

6.   CHAPTER 11, Pg. 53
THE LETTER
Written by WAYNE CARSON THOMPSON
Copyright (c) 1967 BUDDE SONGS, INC.
Used by permission.
All rights reserved

7. CHAPTER 12, Pg. 59
SPACE ODDITY
Words and Music by DAVID BOWIE
© Copyright 1969 (Renewed) ONWARD MUSIC LTD.,
London, England
TRO-Essex Music International, Inc., New York, controls all publication
rights for the U.S.A. and Canada
International Copyright Secured   Made in U.S.A.
All Rights Reserved Including Public Performance For Profit
Used by Permission

8. CHAPTER 15, Pg. 75
STAIRWAY TO HEAVEN
Words and Music by JIMMY PAGE and ROBERT PLANT
© 1972 (Renewed) FLAMES OF ALBION MUSIC, INC.
All Rights Administered by WB MUSIC CORP.
Exclusive Print Rights for the World Excluding Europe
Administered by ALFRED MUSIC PUBLISHING CO., INC.
All Rights Reserved

9. CHAPTER 16, Pg. 81
THE SOUND OF SILENCE
Copyright © 1964 PAUL SIMON
Used by permission of the Publisher: PAUL SIMON MUSIC
All Rights Reserved

10. CHAPTER 17, Pg. 87
TRUCKIN'
Words by ROBERT HUNTER
Music by JERRY GARCIA, PHIL LESH and ROBERT WEIR
© 1970 (Renewed) ICE NINE PUBLISHING CO., INC.
All Rights Reserved

11. CHAPTER 17, Pgs. 89-90
SHAME
By REUBEN CROSS and JOHN H. FITCH JR.
© 1977 UNICHAPPELL MUSIC INC. (BMI) and MILLS AND MILLS
MUSIC (BMI)
All Rights Administered by UNICHAPPELL MUSIC INC.
All Rights Reserved

12. CHAPTER 18, Pg. 93
AND SHE WAS
Words and Music by DAVID BYRNE
© 1985 WB MUSIC CORP. and INDEX MUSIC
All Rights Administered by WB MUSIC CORP.
All Rights Reserved

13. CHAPTER 19, Pg. 101
LISTEN TO THE MUSIC
Words and Music by TOM JOHNSTON
© 1972 (Renewed) WARNER-TAMERLANE PUBLISHING CORP.
All Rights Reserved

18. CHAPTER 26, Pg. 139
DANCE TO THE MUSIC
Words and Music by SYLVESTER STEWART
© 1968 (Renewed) MIJAC MUSIC
All rights administered by WARNER-TAMERLANE
PUBLISHING CORP.
All Rights Reserved

19. CHAPTER 26, Pgs. 139-140
ROSALITA (COME OUT TONIGHT)
By BRUCE SPRINGSTEEN
Copyright © 1974 BRUCE SPRINGSTEEN,
renewed © 2002 BRUCE SPRINGSTEEN (ASCAP)
Reprints by permission. International copyright secured.
All Rights Reserved

20. CHAPTER 31, Pg. 159
LIKE A ROLLING STONE
Words and Music by BOB DYLAN
Copyright © 1965 by WARNER BROS. INC.;
renewed 1993 by SPECIAL RIDER MUSIC
All Rights Reserved

21. CHAPTER 32, Pg. 163
I CAN SEE FOR MILES
Words and Music by PETER TOWNSHEND
© Copyright 1967 (Renewed) FABULOUS MUSIC LTD., London, England
TRO - Essex Music, Inc., New York, controls all publication rights for the
U.S.A. and Canada
International Copyright Secured, Made In U.S.A.
All Rights Reserved Including Public Performance For Profit Used by Permission

22. CHAPTER 32, Pgs. 163-164
JUST WHAT I NEEDED
Words and Music by RIC OCASEK
© 1978 LIDO MUSIC, INC.
All Rights Reserved

23. CHAPTER 32, Pgs. 165-166
YOU'RE ALL I'VE GOT TONIGHT
Words and Music by RIC OCASEK
© 1978 LIDO MUSIC, INC.
All Rights Reserved

24. CHAPTER 34, Pgs. 173-175
TENTH AVENUE FREEZE-OUT
By BRUCE SPRINGSTEEN
Copyright © 1975 BRUCE SPRINGSTEEN,
renewed © 2003 BRUCE SPRINGSTEEN (ASCAP)
Reprinted by permission. International copyright secured.
All rights reserved

25. CHAPTER 39, Pg. 195
RAMBLIN' MAN
Words and Music by DICKEY BETTS
© 1973 (Renewed) UNICHAPPELL MUSIC INC. and FORREST
RICHARD BETTS MUSIC
All Rights Administered by UNICHAPPELL MUSIC, INC.
All Rights Reserved

26. CHAPTER 42, Pg. 207
ALREADY GONE
Words and Music by JACK TEMPCHIN and ROBB STRANDLUND
© 1973 (Renewed) WB MUSIC CORP. and JAZZ BIRD MUSIC
All Rights Administered by WB MUSIC CORP.
All Rights Reserved

27. CHAPTER 43, Pg. 211
EAGLES FLY
By SAMMY HAGAR
© 1987 WB MUSIC CORP. (ASCAP)
All Rights Reserved

28. CHAPTER 44, Pg. 213
I FEEL FREE
Words and Music by JACK BRUCE and PETER BROWN
© 1967 (Renewed) DRATLEAF MUSIC, LTD.
All Rights Administered by UNICHAPPELL MUSIC, INC.
All Rights Reserved

29. EPILOGUE, Pgs. 219-220
INTO THE MYSTIC
Words and Music by VAN MORRISON
© 1970 (Renewed) WB MUSIC CORP. and CALEDONIA
SOUL MUSIC
All Rights Administered by WB MUSIC CORP.
All Rights Reserved